RAZOR

Steel Patriots MC

Book SEVEN

Mary Kennedy

III
INSATIABLE INK

CHAPTER ONE

Diego "Razor" Salcedo, United States Navy SEAL, officially assigned to submarine special warfare command, now stood before the panel of men given the task to judge him and his teammates on the actions taken during their most recent mission. Men, whom he believed had no right to pass judgment given that they were not present, nor had any of them ever done the job his team was required to do.

He shifted, trying to catch a breeze anywhere beneath his uniform, the heat oppressive in the small meeting room. *Judge away,* he thought to himself. If you think you would have done anything different, then you are not the men you claim to be. His thoughts were direct and charged with anger. Desperately wanting to speak out against them, he chewed on the inside of his mouth to prevent himself from saying something stupid.

Diego, in his job, was calm, cool, and always in control. Personally? Not so much sometimes. His Latin blood boiled to the surface on more than one occasion, and he regretted it. The first time was in fourth grade when Grady Perkins pushed him on the playground. He made sure Grady understood that he would push back. Grady got detention. Diego was suspended for a day for punching another student. He really didn't care about that as much as he did the end of his abuela's hand on his backside. That hurt more than anything.

The next time was high school when Malcolm White told him that 'no Mexican' was going to date his sister. Hell, he didn't even want to date Regina White. He was just going to take her to the prom because they both didn't have dates and were friends. But old Malcolm had to open his mouth, earning him a broken nose. Yea, good thing it was his senior year.

He floundered after school, working construction jobs and landscaping until the day he got the call that his abuela had died. His whole world crumbled that day. No consistency, no rules, no one to go home to. He wandered into the recruitment office and said, "I want to join the Marines." When the recruiter said he wasn't "fit enough" to be a Marine, he left and went to the Navy recruiter. Six months later, he was through basic and determined to become a Navy SEAL.

After failing the first time, he returned for a second try, determined to prove that the Marine recruiter was an ass. He graduated at the top of his class. He returned to that recruiter's office with his trident gleaming on his uniform, flipping him the bird.

That's how he met Eric "Ghost" Stanton, his team lead. They'd connected immediately, Ghost admiring his fighting style, using his long, lean, wiry frame to his advantage with men bigger than him. What Ghost especially admired were his skills with a knife.

Now, nearly twelve years later, he was sitting before a panel of morons with more ribbons than brains, judging him for killing the filth that tortured and killed twelve little girls. Did he use excessive force? Yep. Did he slit their throats before the building was set to blow? Yep. Did he regret it? Nope.

He was a United States Navy SEAL. The most elite warriors known to man, and he was proud to serve on a team of like-minded elite warriors from all branches of service. The team led by Eric "Ghost" Stanton, also a SEAL, was made up of SEALs, Army Rangers, and MARSOC, all the best trained, the most feared warriors of their class. Each man hand-selected by Ghost to serve on a team where they would be called to perform missions others could not do or refused to do. Their record was stellar, their success rate one hundred percent. Until this mission.

This mission, they'd received spotty intelligence and communication from an Army intelligence officer who was not their normal conduit for intel. This guy looked as though he'd barely finished boot camp, and the way he hung his head at the table indicated to Razor that he knew he was partly at fault for the poor information.

He tried to wait patiently for the men to speak, killing the time by reciting his credo:

In times of war or uncertainty, there is a special breed of warrior ready to answer our Nation's call. A common man with uncommon desire to succeed.

Forged by adversity, he stands alongside America's finest special operations forces to serve his country, the American people, and protect their way of life.

I am that man.

My Trident is a symbol of honor and heritage. Bestowed upon me by the heroes that have gone before, it embodies the trust of those I have sworn to protect. By wearing the Trident, I accept the responsibility of my chosen profession and way of life. It is a privilege that I must earn every day.

My loyalty to Country and Team is beyond reproach. I humbly serve as a guardian to my fellow Americans always ready to defend those who are unable to defend themselves. I do not advertise the nature of my work, nor seek recognition for my actions. I voluntarily accept the inherent hazards of my profession, placing the welfare and security of others before my own.

I serve with honor on and off the battlefield. The ability to control my emotions and my actions, regardless of circumstance, sets me apart from other men.

Uncompromising integrity is my standard. My character and honor are steadfast. My word is my bond.

We expect to lead and be led. In the absence of orders, I will take charge, lead my teammates and accomplish the mission. I lead by example in all situations.

I will never quit. I persevere and thrive on adversity. My Nation expects me to be physically harder and mentally stronger than my enemies. If knocked down, I will get back up, every time. I will draw on every remaining ounce of strength to protect my teammates and to accomplish our mission. I am never out of the fight.

We demand discipline. We expect innovation. The lives of my teammates and the success of our mission depend on me – my technical skill, tactical proficiency, and attention to detail. My training is never complete.

We train for war and fight to win. I stand ready to bring the full spectrum of combat power to bear in order to achieve my mission and the goals established by my country. The execution of my duties will be swift and violent when required yet guided by the very principles that I serve to defend.

Brave men have fought and died building the proud tradition and feared reputation that I am bound to uphold. In the worst of conditions, the legacy of my teammates steadies my resolve and silently guides my every deed.

I will not fail.

"Chief Salcedo, do you believe that your team acted in the best interests of the mission?" asked Admiral Crossing.

"I do, sir. We were tasked with rescuing those girls. We were *told* it was a kidnapping for ransom, but what we discovered was that it was something far worse. If you had seen those girls hanging on that cliff, beaten, raped, and tortured, I highly doubt you would have acted differently."

"And do you believe your team lead acted appropriately?" he asked.

"I believe that Master Chief Stanton acted with the highest integrity, sir, and I would follow him anywhere." The eyebrows rose at the table, and Diego stared down each man. He meant every word of it.

"Do you have any regrets, Chief Salcedo?" said Admiral Crossing.

"None," said Razor.

"Thank you," said Crossing. "You can step outside and wait with your teammates while we finish with the others."

Razor stepped into the hallway pulling at his collar, sweat rolling down the back of his neck. He looked at his teammates and murmured "lazy fucking brass" as he took his seat. He waited as each man told his story, and then Jack "Doc" Harris was called.

Because of the shitty construction of the building, they could hear everything being said inside the room, and when Jack "Doc" Harris notified the members of the panel that he possessed photos of the girls, they all stirred a bit in their seats. Taking photos of prisoners, dead bodies, anything to do with a mission was strictly forbidden unless directed to do so. Doc could be placing a noose on all their necks, or he could be saving them.

Doc stepped outside the room and stared at his teammates, nodding at them to walk with him to the end of the hallway.

"Fucking hell, Doc, we didn't know you had photos," said Ghost.

"I know. I took them when we were cutting the girls down. Don't ask me why. I know it's a violation, but I just had this feeling, and shit for luck, it paid off."

"Well," said Razor, "I, for one, am fucking eternally grateful. They won't court-martial us with the fear of those photos becoming public. The liberals would be screaming about human rights, and the conservatives would say the killing of those men was justified. They don't want to have to argue that."

"This shit is getting fucking exhausting," said Ghost. "I'm so damned tired of having to follow rules created by men who don't do the damn job anymore or, for that matter, ever did the job." They all nodded as the doors of the hearing room opened once again. The MP waved them inside.

Standing before the committee, the men all removed their hats and stood at attention.

"Gentlemen, you have presented us with a dilemma, and I won't lie, it's one I hate," said Admiral Crossing. "Your work as a unit has been indisputable, but we are getting pressures from the country's government claiming you murdered innocent men.

"I didn't say I agree. However, we are tasked with making a show of, hell, I don't even know anymore. We are asking you to retire, gentlemen. If you refuse, you will be dishonorably discharged. If you take the retirement, there will be no mark on your records. It saddens me to do this, to lose some of the finest men I know and that I know we need in our service."

"I accept retirement," said Razor. Shit. Thirty-three years old, and he was going to be retired.

The chorus was heard down the line as each man agreed, regrettably. The Admiral nodded at them, handing them their papers that would tell administration they were taking retirement effective immediately.

"You will be expected to be packed and on the next transport home within forty-eight hours. I wish you good luck, men. The world needs people like you. I hope you find a way to continue to the good fight."

Thirty-three hours later, they were seated in the back of a transport on their way home. Their bags packed, their papers in hand, and no clue what they would do next. Seven of the most elite, deadliest warriors ever to serve out of a job.

"Where will you go, Ghost?" asked Whiskey. Ghost looked at the men he'd called teammates for the last decade. Each man was hand-selected for his team, partly because he knew of their skills but mostly because he trusted them with his life and the lives of every member of the team.

"I have a proposition for all of you. I know some of you have family back home, but nobody has an old lady that I'm aware of," he said, smirking at the men on the transport.

"Well, Tango has a mule he's fond of," said Doc with a smile.

"Fuck you, Doc, at least it's a female mule," he grinned. "So, what's your point, Ghost?"

"My point is, when my pops died, he left me a huge piece of land. It's nothing special, but it's got an old garage on the property where he used to repair cars, bikes, tractors, shit like that for neighbors. The house burned down years ago, but Pops made the barn into a pretty livable space."

"SOOO, you want us all to live there?" asked Gunner.

"Like share bunk beds or some shit?" questioned Zulu.

"No, I mean, yea. Look, I ride. You all know that, and I know that most of you do too. What if we formed our own club, motorcycle club? We pick a name, make the garage something that we can all work, and maybe open a bar or some shit."

The men all looked at one another, nodding. It was a good idea, but not one of them knew anything about running a business or a bar.

"I'm in," said Tango, "but I know jack-shit about operating a bar. I can fix anything with a motor, and so can most of you but a bar? I don't know, man. I know *how* to drink, just not how to mix drinks."

"Look, it doesn't have to happen right away. MCs are pretty territorial. We need to make sure we're not stepping on anyone's toes. I'm not a fan of becoming an outlaw MC. We got our taste of outlaw in that fucking shithole we just came from, and it didn't do any of us any good. I'm suggesting that between the bar and the garage, we'll have two legitimate businesses. Maybe on the side, we sort of informally help people."

"Help people? Like good Samaritans?" asked Gunner.

"Sort of, I'm thinking more like we take jobs others won't, but only the ones we want to take. We find lost kids, kidnap victims. We help the old lady being screwed over by a nasty landlord, shit like that." The men all looked at him, raising their eyebrows. "Look, I know we've spent our entire careers doing just this kind of shit, but now we get to do it on our terms. The shop needs cleaning up, and the barn will need to be made inhabitable – adding more electrical, plumbing – but it's huge. I've got a shit ton of money saved from all my deployments, and Pops left me a nice little chunk of change."

"And we'd be partners?" asked Whiskey.

"Yea, we'd be fucking partners. We'd be brothers, asshole," he said with a grin. "Just like we are now. We'd rely on one another and do shit our way. No red tape, no governments telling us what to do. We ride our fucking bikes when we want. We take the jobs we want. We fuck who we want, and we drink 'til we can't drink no more." The men smiled in his direction.

"I'm in," said Tango.

"Me too," said Doc.

"Why the fuck not?" said Razor.

"Fuck, you know I'm in, asshole," said Gunner.

"I guess we need a name," said Whiskey. "How about Steel Soldiers?"

"No fucking way, asshole. I'm a SEAL, not a fucking soldier," said Tango. The others laughed and nodded. They were all from different branches of the military and loved teasing each other about the superiority of their own branch, but deep down held mad respect for one another.

"Steel Patriots," said Ghost. "The steel between our legs and the fucking patriot spirit we all still carry."

"Steel Patriots," whispered Whiskey. The others nodded and smiled.

"Steel Patriots it is."

CHAPTER TWO

Razor looked in the mirror at his reflection. The black suit and tie, so vastly different from his usual work clothes of jeans and a t-shirt. This last mission cost him something very important, something fragile, something difficult to replace – his humanity. Sitting in that fucking prison, acting as a concerned counselor and therapist to murderers, drug addicts, sex offenders, and the worst – child molesters, nearly broke him.

He did it for his teammate Tango and his woman, Taylor. He did it to ensure that her stepbrother would never see the light of day again. What he was struggling with was why the justice system allowed him to occupy valuable air, valuable real estate on this planet when he clearly didn't deserve to be here.

When they'd formulated the plan to remove Evan Black from any future equations, he wasn't bothered by it in the least. He was thrilled that their plan worked. Now what he was struggling with were the images that he'd painted in his mind. The images he couldn't erase of what he'd done not only to Taylor but to other women. Images that Evan was happy to share in painful detail.

He loosened the tie, removing it, placing it on his dresser. Then taking off the starched white shirt, he tossed it in the laundry pile, then hung up the suit where it would gather dust for another year until the next wedding or funeral.

Pulling on his jeans and t-shirt, he heard the soft knock on his door and debated whether or not to open it. Looking out the window of the guest cottage he occupied for now, he saw Taylor and Tango.

"Hey, beautiful," he said, plastering the smile on his face. "How are you?"

"I'm great," she said, smiling back. "Do you have a minute for me, Razor?"

"Uh, yea, sure, come on in." Taylor walked through the door, and Tango just stood there. He shook his head.

"Just her, brother, she needs to talk to you. I'll wait right here." Razor nodded at his friend, frowning. Jesus, did Taylor have something horrible to say.

"Have a seat," he said, sitting on the sofa.

"This won't take long, I promise," she said, smiling at him. "Razor, I-I wanted to thank you for what you did for me." She lifted her hands when he started to blow it off as nothing and shook her head.

"Please, let me finish. What you did was what any of you would have done, I know that. It's how you're all hard-wired, how you work. You save the world without a second thought. I mean, look at you guys. You're retired, and yet you form a motorcycle club that still helps the little guys, the underdog. That says a lot about you.

"What I know, though, is you heard a lot, Razor. You heard Evan say things. Things about what he did to me, to those other girls. I can only imagine how difficult that was for you, how hard it was to sit there listening to him."

Razor looked down at his folded hands. He couldn't look in those blue eyes and let her know that he heard it all. He heard the hideous, horrible things her own stepbrother did to her.

"Look at me, Razor, please," she pleaded. He looked up and immediately felt the emotion cloud his throat. "It's okay, Razor. It's okay for you to know what he did to me. It doesn't define me. It damn sure doesn't define you. We are not him. We are not sick; we are not demented. If anyone had to know about it all, I'm glad it was you."

He jerked his head, looking up at her. She was glad he heard that sick shit?

"You don't judge people, Razor. I've watched you. You have no bias toward anyone. I don't know how you do it. You met with those men and heard those horrible things, yet you still found humanity in it all. You found the good in a man like Castro. Who else but you could do that?"

"I'm... I'm not sure..."

"I want you to let it go," she said, grabbing his hand. "I need for you to let it go for me, but also for you and for your brothers. People like Evan will always exist, Razor. We know that, but we will stop them. He is not worth your mental health. Let. It. Go. Fill your head with beautiful thoughts, not Evan. Erase his name from your mind. I know I will."

"I don't know if I can," he whispered. Taylor rose to sit next to him, wrapping a tiny arm around his shoulders. She kissed his cheek.

"You have to. I need for you to be the godfather of my child when we get pregnant. I need for you to be happy and healthy, and more than anything, I need for you to be here for your teammates. They need you more than you know."

"Wh-what children?"

"Who else would I choose, Razor? You're the man who risked everything to go into that prison. Not just your body, but something far more precious, your mind, your soul. I know that you will be able to wipe it away and live a life worth living."

"My brother should be damn glad he got you before I did and that I love him. Otherwise, I'd be stealing you away, Taylor," he said, kissing her cheek. She smiled, nodding.

"Well, don't tell Tango, but if he had let me go, I was coming for you," she winked.

"I heard that!" yelled the voice on the porch. They both chuckled and stood from the sofa. Razor pulled her in for a long hug, grateful that she was healthy and alive and he could hug her.

"Thank you for coming here, Taylor."

"Thank you for making sure I can live my life. Now do me a favor?" He looked at her quizzically. "Live yours, Razor. Go out and find that someone who melts your heart, that makes you believe again. You deserve it more than anyone I know."

Razor nodded as they walked to the front door. Tango was leaning against the doorframe, grinning at the other man.

"You good, brother?"

"I'm good, man, thanks."

"Come on," said Tango. "Ghost wants to talk to all of us." Razor nodded as he pulled his front door closed, looking at the small crucifix on his wall. He smiled, looking up at his abuela.

CHAPTER THREE

The men gathered around the big kitchen table to ensure that any loose ends regarding Evan Black were tied off and buried. The warden guaranteed there would be no ties to the Steel Patriots, nor would there be any backlash to the fictional Dr. John Diaz, but nevertheless, they were being cautious.

"Do you think we need to worry about Gavin Baker?" asked Ghost, staring at Razor.

"Yes, no, I don't know, man. I know I can't let Castro's sister be out there on her own while he's still free. He's violated his parole, so there's a BOLO and warrant out for him, but they're not gonna waste a lot of manpower. As far as we know, he didn't make any calls to the prison or speak with Black once he was released, but we don't know if they communicated through some other means or made some sort of pact.

"I know Castro is just some gang member who killed other gang members, but at his core, he did everything for all the right reasons, and there's a piece of me that respects him."

"Understandable," said Tango. "We all know what it's like to protect those we love. Seems to me he was just a kid himself, suddenly in charge of his kid sister. I'm not saying I agree with what he did, but I understand why he did it, and let's be honest, almost every one of us could say we killed at least six 'gang' members or 'Taliban' members or whatever the shit label you want to put on it."

"Alright, let's just watch out and just make sure we're checking in with the DS boys. Are Shred and Crash on their way home?"

"Yea, man," said Razor. "Shred said he might head toward Tech just to make sure he didn't spot his brother. Figures if he's there, he might try to come for him and leave the girl alone."

"Dude is solid, man," said Tango. "I mean, he's willing to let that lunatic come after him instead of a girl he doesn't even know." Razor nodded once again.

Darby walked into the kitchen with Calla right on her heels, the long brown curls held back today in a purple and gold bow, her little blue jeans and sweater with her chucks making her look older than she was. Razor couldn't help but smile. She was the cutest little thing in the world. With the other babies all being boys right now, she was the princess of the group.

"Uncle Tango!" she yelled, leaping into his arms.

"Hey, pretty girl," he said, kissing her cheek with a wet raspberry. "What are you doing today?"

"Mommy said since it's Saturday, I can go to the store with her for a while."

"Why you goin' to the store, babe?" asked Gunner.

"I told you," she said with her hands on her hips. Gunner wanted to say he remembered. He just truly did not. "The guy who writes those books about motorcycles and motorcycle trips? Really? Geez, Gunner, you guys were the ones who asked me to carry them. He's coming into the store. Turns out he lives only a few hours away. We want to talk about doing a book signing for his new book coming out this month, *Adventures in Color – Touring in the Fall on Your Bike*. It's beautiful! All these amazing pictures of places he toured last fall. He started up in Canada and worked his way down. It's stunning!"

"Damn, Darby!" said Ghost. "You got him to do a book signing?"

"That's what we're talking about," she said, nodding. "I'm hoping he'll be the first of many. It could be a really big deal for the bookstore. Come on, Calla. Gotta go!" She kissed Gunner as he slapped her behind. Darby jumped with a little yelp.

"Go wait in the restaurant, baby," she said, turning back toward Gunner. She walked back toward him as he leaned against the cupboard, his long legs crossed at his ankles. For a minute, he was worried she might be pissed. Instead, she reached her delicate hand toward him, rubbing it up and down his semi-hard length. Standing on her tiptoes, she let her tongue follow the line of his mouth.

"Keep that in mind for tonight, big boy," she grinned, turning and winking at the other men. Gunner swallowed, straightening himself.

"Holy shit, that was fucking hot," said Tango.

"That's what I'm talking about," said Ghost. "That's the kind of shit happening in my house too!" Hawk and Eagle stood, shaking their heads together.

"Read the fucking books!"

CHAPTER FOUR

Razor made sure that he kept in touch with the two men guarding Isabella Castro. Although there was nothing to report, he felt a strong need to ensure that he followed through on his promise to Castro. He spoke to the man twice through the warden, and he was grateful that he'd kept his promise about his sister.

The weeks following the deaths of Evan and Louis Black, Razor was finally able to concentrate on his true love. The building of their custom motorcycles. He'd found an avenue for all his anger by pouring his emotions into the custom paintwork on the machines he loved. His creativity seemed to be sparked by anything and everything. Some days he would just pull a tank off the shelf and start sketching, no rhyme or reason, no customer in mind. From the tank, Tango or Skull would get inspired, and a bike would be born.

As Halloween got closer, the team closed one Sunday and took the entire group to a pumpkin farm where they rode hayrides, picked apples, and, of course, bought pumpkins.

The twin boys dressed as Oompa Loompas from the movie *Charlie and the Chocolate Factory*. JT dressed as Prince Charming with Calla as his princess. It was adorable. Bree and Kat were both over their morning sickness and both already sporting little basketballs for bellies. Taylor ceremoniously announced her pregnancy loudly, and Razor could not have been happier for her and Tango.

He smiled as he heard his teammates discussing the books the women were reading. Grace, who had a love of romance novels, and it appeared erotic, almost pornographic romance novels, shared the books with all the women, which, it seemed, prompted some romantic, unexpected evenings for the men.

Hawk and Eagle read the books religiously when the girls were through, trying to gain knowledge of the fairer and, obviously, smarter sex. The others either read the discarded books or downloaded them on tablets or e-readers. Razor thought they should all be grateful and just accept it, but they wanted in on the secret, and now all were reading the novels.

"Did you read the first book?" asked Gunner quietly.

"I finished it last night on my tablet," said Ghost. "Some of that shit is pornographic! I'm telling you, I was so hard at one point I thought I would embarrass myself on the sofa next to Grace."

"You didn't like it?" asked Zulu, staring at this friend.

"Loved that fucking shit!" growled Ghost. The others laughed, nodding.

"Okay then, let's keep reading because I can tell you for damn sure there were some things in that book that I had to stop and think about positioning to get my head wrapped around it. I will be doing some of that shit," said Tango.

Ace walked toward the group, nodding at Razor. Ace was a different breed from the rest. A warrior, a veteran, and an avid rider, but he was awkward and shy, almost dysfunctional. He rarely touched people, and when he did, it was for the briefest moment.

"They still talking about the romance books?" he asked, looking confused. Razor chuckled, shaking his head.

"Yea, what's up, man?" he asked.

"Shred from DS is on the line for you. Says it's about Isabella Castro." Razor nodded, following Ace to the communications room, Tango and Ghost close behind. Placing the phone on speaker, he addressed the other man.

"Shred? It's Razor, brother. What's up?"

"My fucking brother is what's up," he said, sounding winded.

"You okay?" asked Ghost.

"Yea, I'm... damn, that fucking hurts!" They could hear a woman speaking in the background, and the sounds of medical equipment beeping, calls being made.

"Are you in the fucking hospital?" asked Razor.

"Yea, bastard got the drop on me. Stabbed me in the side, but I'm gonna be fine if this damn doctor will stop poking me!" he yelled. Ghost and Razor grinned.

"What about Isabella? Is she okay?" asked Razor, suddenly very concerned.

"She is man, but she's shaken up. He had her pinned in her apartment. She was terrified when we finally got in there. She's not harmed, but she doesn't want to be alone. I can stay..."

"I'm on my way," said Razor, walking out of the room. Tango and Ghost followed him with their eyes.

"Did he just say he was on his way?" asked Shred.

"Uh, yea, man, he's on his way. You need me to call Whitey?" asked Ghost.

"No, Crash called him. I'm fine. Really, I am, Ghost. Crash is sitting with Isabella at our hotel. Once I'm cleared, I'll take a cab and meet them. She'll be safe until Razor gets here."

"Okay, man, thanks. What do we do about your brother?"

"Oh, that's easy. I'm hunting his ass down and killing him."

CHAPTER FIVE

"Razor? Brother, you don't have to drive down there. They have the situation under control," said Ghost.

"I know, man, but I made this promise, and I'm going to see it through until we find this guy. I can't imagine the terror that woman was feeling. She's blind, man. Fucking blind and that son-of-a-bitch had her cornered in her apartment like an animal."

"Razor? Brother, look at me," said Ghost softly, then more forcefully. "Chief!" Razor stopped and turned, staring at his friend and lead.

"Sorry."

"Razor, you do not have to kill yourself on this. You're exhausted, brother, burning the shit at both ends. That prison gig took a lot out of you. We can send someone to get the girl if you want to bring her back here, but you need to think about this. She's a young blind woman used to trying to be independent. She's familiar with her home, the campus, everything, and now you're going to remove her and bring her here."

Razor frowned at Ghost, stepping back from his duffel. He ran a hand through his dark hair, gripping his neck in an attempt to relieve the pressure and stress.

"It will be okay. I'll go down, assess the situation, and then make the call. But if Baker is still free, she's in danger. Hell, even if he's not, Castro has enemies, and she could still be in trouble. I can't let that poor young woman be left vulnerable."

"You like this woman?" asked Tango.

"I don't know her, brother. Never met her, don't know what she looks like. I just know I need to do this," he said, looking at his friends. Ghost finally nodded.

"Keep your fucking phone on and call or text the minute you arrive and when you leave. I'm not fucking with you, Razor. If I don't hear from you, I'll send the whole damn team down there after you." He nodded, continuing to pack his bag as Tango gripped his shoulder.

"You call me for anything, brother, and I do mean anything." Razor nodded, not looking up as he slung the bag over his shoulder and headed out.

The drive to Atlanta was eight to nine hours on a good day. Razor did it in seven and a half, and it was raining cats and dogs. And not a nice summer rain. No, this shit was cold and pelting. He was eternally grateful that he'd driven his truck.

Arriving at the hotel outside of Atlanta, he looked at his watch, two in the morning. He was tired, hungry, and pissed off. They'd done everything they could to protect Castro's sister. Somehow Gavin Baker still got to her. Obviously, despite the fact that Evan Black was dead, Gavin was going to follow through with his promise to harm the girl to make Castro suffer.

He tapped on the door that Shred and Crash had indicated, and the other man opened the door, waving him inside.

"Where is she?" he asked. Shred pressed a finger to his lips, effectively silencing him.

"She's in the adjoining room. We left the door connecting us cracked, but she needed her own space, brother." Razor nodded at the other man.

"You okay?"

"Will be," he said, letting out a loud hiss as he lay down again. "My brother learned a few tricks in prison. He's changed a bit, but I'll give you all the details in the morning. Get some sleep, man. You look exhausted."

Razor took the other bed in his room, crashing immediately. His head was spinning with what he had to do tomorrow or, technically, today. He needed to convince Isabella Castro to let him take her somewhere safe. Yet, he knew she would most likely object. Closing his eyes, he finally drifted off to sleep.

As light filtered into the room, he felt something cold and wet against his cheek. Brushing it away, he turned and then felt a sudden weight against the bed and his side. He jumped to his feet, reaching for his weapon as the huge dog tilted his head, staring at him.

"Fucking hell," he said, letting out a long breath.

"Taco?" He heard the breathy, sultry voice and stilled. "Taco, where are you, boy?" Holy shit, who was that? No. No, God wouldn't do this to me, he thought. He wouldn't make this woman have that sexy voice, not Castro's sister. It was like whiskey being filtered through velvet, smooth, intoxicating, and so damned sexy he couldn't help it when his dick jumped.

She pushed open the door calling once more, her voluptuous body exposed to him in the morning light.

"Taco, are you in here, boy?" She stilled immediately, her heading lifting, knowing that there was someone else in this room besides her and Taco. "Crash, is that you?"

Razor was glued to the carpet. Isabella Castro was a fucking bombshell. Long dark brown hair, big brown eyes with the thickest black lashes he'd ever seen. Her hourglass body was made for loving, curves he could grip and grind against, her tits easily double Ds made his mouth water. But her ass, that beautiful, plump juicy ass made him ache.

"This isn't funny," she said in a weak voice, fear etched with pain directed at him.

"I-I'm sorry," he said. Her head turned quickly toward his voice, shock filling her delicate features as he spoke.

"Wh-who are you? Taco!" She called for the dog once again, who immediately sat next to her, her hand touching his head for reassurance.

"It's okay, Isabella. It's okay. I know your brother, Hector. He asked me to make sure you were safe from this man, Gavin Baker. The man who attacked you yesterday."

"And do you have a name, friend of my brother's?" she said, smiling, relaxing somewhat in her stance next to the dog.

"Oh, shit, sorry, yea, I'm Razor. I mean, my friends call me Razor, but my name is Diego Salcedo."

"Diego," she said, grinning. "I like both those names. Razor is very edgy, dangerous. Diego is sexy. Are you sexy, Razor?" He nearly fell to his knees. Yea, I'm fucking sexy; my dick is huge and rock hard. I want to strip that sweet body and lick you from head to toe; yea, I'm sexy, and I want to sex you up, beautiful.

"I-I guess I'm okay," he said, grinning and then realizing she couldn't see his grin. In fact, it suddenly hit him that all his physical attributes that he used to lure women in wouldn't work. He couldn't use one of his killer smiles, his trademark gazes, or his moves on the dance floor. What the fuck was he supposed to do now?

"Can I touch your face, Diego? May I feel what you look like?" she asked.

"Y-yes," he said, clearing his throat. He stepped closer to her, stopping within arm's length, but Isabella moved a step closer, her breasts now touching his chest; she took a deep breath and exhaled. He nearly groaned aloud, his cock instantly jumping.

She lay her long, lean fingers against his face, delicately tracing the lines of his jaw, gliding one long index finger down his nose, following the curve of his lips, and back up to his eyes. Her touch was cool and gentle, the neatly trimmed nails slightly grazing his skin. Then she let both hands glide through his hair, gripping him tightly.

What the fuck was happening here, he thought. Was she going to kiss him? How in the hell would he explain this to Castro? Suddenly, she pulled his head within inches of her sweet mouth, and he waited. He was so distracted; it took him a moment to register what she'd done. Her knee connected to his groin, his balls shriveling up inside him, his semi-hard cock now painfully soft. He moaned and doubled over, gasping for air.

"What in the hell! Why did you do that?" he shouted.

"Tell my hermano I don't want his drug-selling, crime-ridden vermin protecting me. I can do it myself."

"What the fuck, lady! I'm not a drug-selling… forget it. Get your shit. We're leaving."

"I'm not going anywhere with you!" she yelled as she headed to the other room. She tried to slam the door, but Razor was there to push it back. She stumbled, unable to catch her balance, and he reached, catching her waist and pulling her to him. Dear lord, all those fucking curves melted against his body.

"Let me go!" she yelled.

"No, you have to come with me, or this man will be back for you."

"Fuck off!"

"Listen to me!" he yelled, shaking her shoulders slightly. "Listen!" Isabella stilled at the feeling of his strong hands gripping her shoulders. This man smelled delicious. It was a mix of leather, cologne, and something else – motor oil. Damn!

"Listen to me, Bella."

"Don't call me that."

"Listen, Gavin Baker is a psychotic, murdering sex offender. He is going to come for you to get back at your brother. I made a promise, and

I damned sure never go back on my promises. I will do everything in my power to keep you safe until this lunatic is caught. Now, you have twenty minutes to gather your shit, or I will do it for you." Razor watched as her chest rose and fell, the smooth caramel skin visible from the open neck of her t-shirt, those breasts screaming at him.

Isabella could hear the concern in the man's voice, but she had no clue if he was telling the truth or not. He smelled sexy; he sounded sexy and sincere, but she couldn't rely on those things. And if he were a friend of her brother's, she didn't want any part in that. She heard the door open and waited.

"I see you two have met," said Crash, smiling.

"Hey, man," said Razor with an exhaustion he didn't know he possessed. "Can you please tell the princess I'm not some lunatic, and I'm here to help." Crash laughed, nodding his head.

"Yea, man. Hey, listen, Izzy, he's a stand-up dude. He is who he says he is. Trust him, beautiful. He'll make sure you're kept safe from this insanity." Isabella crossed her arms under her breasts, those huge brown eyes searching the room but not seeing.

"And how do I know for sure that you're not all crazy? That you're not all criminals just trying to kill me?" she said with a huff.

"Because if I wanted you dead, beautiful," said Razor, "you'd already be dead. Now get your shit together. I'm running thin on patience and sleep. I can do without the sleep, but I can assure you that you cannot do without my patience."

"Uh, why don't we grab breakfast and talk about this," said Shred.

"Fine," said Razor in a huff. "I'll be at the diner. Bring her pretty little ass over when she's ready and throw her shit in my truck. We leave after breakfast."

CHAPTER SIX

"Who in the hell does he think he is?" asked Isabella. Both men looked at one another, watching as Razor took long strides across the parking lot to the diner. "If he thinks I'm going with him, he's crazy!"

"Listen, Izzy, he's a stand-up dude. You really don't have a choice, honey. Baker got to you last night easily, and without one of us here or that man, I'm afraid of what might happen to you. Swallow your pride, woman. He's going to need to help you, and you're going to need his help in order to keep you alive."

Isabella swallowed and tried to hold back the tears threatening to spill. Finally nodding, she threw what few items she brought with her into the bag, asked the other men to grab Taco's food and toys, and then grabbed the harness on Taco.

Entering the diner, Shred led her to the big booth where Razor was seated. Razor stood and guided her into the seat against the window. The dog lay dutifully at her feet, his big, sweet head nuzzled against her legs. Razor slid in beside her and felt her stiffen, Crash and Shred on the other side of the booth.

"What'll it be?" asked the waitress.

"Just coffee and toast for me," said Shred.

"Coffee and the western omelet for me," said Crash.

"Same," said Razor.

"And for you, honey?" asked the woman. Isabella hesitated for a moment, the others not realizing why she waited. Clearing her throat, she finally asked.

"Do you have a braille menu?" she asked. The woman looked up at her, almost thinking she was joking, then thought better of it seeing the expression on Razor's face.

"Oh, no, hun, I don't. We got eggs any way you want 'em. I got waffles and pancakes, oatmeal, or cereal. You tell me what you want, and I can probably make it happen." Isabella smiled and nodded.

"Thank you, coffee and an egg white omelet with veggies if you have it," she said, smiling.

"Done, sugar, be right back with your coffee." Silence ensued as they waited for their food. Crash was finally the one to break the deafening roar.

"So, what's the plan here? Do we need to keep tracking Baker?" he asked.

"He's my fucking brother, and he's a lunatic, so yea, I'm gonna track him," said Shred. Isabella's head rose at that.

"He-he's your brother?" she asked nervously. Razor noticed her hands trembling and reached out, covering them with one of his larger hands.

"Yea, beautiful, but believe me, I don't like to claim that shit. Sometimes I think my mom dropped him on his head. I wish it were that easy, but you can be assured I'm out to stop him, not help him." She nodded and wiggled her fingers, then pulled away from the heat of Razor's hand.

He hated that she did. He loved the feeling of his big rough hand on top of her tiny, small fingers. She wasn't a tall woman, maybe five-three or five-four to his six-foot-one, but she was about the most voluptuous woman he'd ever seen, and his dick was definitely taking notice of every fucking curve on her body, even in its bruised state.

"I-I have exams, my work, my classes," she said, suddenly feeling a bit of panic and unsure.

"Can you do them online?" asked Razor. Turning her head slightly toward his voice, she nodded.

"Most of them. I mean, I guess I could ask my professors. Damn, this will delay my PhD. My work I can definitely do online, or they can ship me the braille texts. I hate this!" The food arrived and Isabella smelled the plate placed before her. She waited, as if expecting something else, , and then Isabella sat very still for a minute.

"Do you need something, Bella?" asked Razor.

"Don't call me that," she said through clenched lips. "I-I need to know where the food is on the plate. Like a clock…"

"Your omelet is stretched between seven and ten; the hash browns are between three and five; your toast is at your eleven o'clock, and your coffee and juice are side-by-side at one and two." She nodded and then turned toward him once more.

"Have you done that before?" she asked.

"Nope. Just know clock speak," he grinned. Hell, his entire life in the military surrounded time and the reference of time. Yea, he knew clock speak, and some days he fucking hated that shit.

They ate the rest of their meal in relative silence, but Razor took note of how carefully she ate her food, almost as if she didn't want to embarrass herself by spilling anything. When they were done, she simply pushed the plate aside.

"I need to use the ladies' room," she said, nudging Razor's shoulder. He stood and gripped her elbow, helping her from the seat. Guiding her to the door, he opened it and looked inside.

"Stalls are on the left about ten paces. I'll wait right here for you." Razor waited patiently for the woman wondering how she managed to do all of these things if someone weren't with her. Did she never go anywhere that was unfamiliar? If so, what it would be like for her at the compound. He took out his phone and called Ace.

"Hey, brother," said Ace.

"Hey, man, listen, I'm bringing Isabella back with me. I need to see if we can make sure there's clear paths for her to get everywhere. I'm just realizing that she's new to everything there and won't be comfortable with where anything is."

"I can handle all of that," said Ace. "Does she have a dog?"

"Yea, big fucker too. I'm hoping Bullitt doesn't get this big, or Gunner and Darby are going to have their hands full. He's sweet, though, sticks close to her."

"No worries, man. It will all be good by the time she gets here."

"Thanks, brother," he said, disconnecting the call. The door opened, and Isabella walked out with the dog.

"I want to go home," she said with a slightly trembling lip.

"No can do, beautiful."

"You don't control what I can do. Take me back to my apartment right now!" she said, stomping her foot. Razor let out an exasperated breath, driving his fingers through his hair.

"I don't have time for this shit! Get in the truck," he ordered, pointing at the door as if she could see him.

"I wouldn't get in your damn truck even if I could see it to get into it, so, no!"

"Fine, we do it your way," he said. Bending at the waist, he tossed Isabella over his shoulder, walking through the diner waving at everyone. "See you brothers later. Shred? Let me know if you see your brother."

"Good luck, man," he chuckled.

"Let me down!" she called. Poor Taco was racing in circles, not sure whether to bark or not. Razor slapped her ass hard and then immediately regretted it. That slap, the feel of her beautiful ass beneath his fingers made his dick rock-hard.

Opening the door, he set her in the passenger seat, shoving her long hair from her face, and then buckled her in. Calling the dog, he jumped up and into the back seat of the truck.

"Let me go!" she yelled again. Razor did the only thing he could to shut her up. He kissed her.

CHAPTER SEVEN

Isabella was quiet for the next twenty minutes, her fingers lightly playing over her lips. Razor regretted the kiss almost immediately. That's not true; he didn't regret the kiss one fucking bit. What he regretted were the feelings the kiss evoked. Isabella Castro was fucking hot. Her body was made for a man to play with, her hips full and curvy, her thighs strong. Her small waist was perfect to grip, and those damned breasts pressed against his back almost made him embarrass himself.

But the kiss, the fucking kiss, was what lit the fire for him. Her soft lips felt untouched, and he couldn't help but wonder if she'd ever kissed anyone before. She was twenty-eight years old and to expect her to be a virgin seemed absurd, yet she kissed like a virgin with uncertainty and inexperience.

Driving down the freeway, he touched his own lips and moaned. Her head turned slightly, and he stilled, realizing that she would hear all the subtle changes in his body.

"Wh-why did you kiss me?"

"To shut you up," he said. He regretted the words almost immediately. "And because I wanted to."

"Why?" she asked, staring straight ahead.

"You're a beautiful woman, Isabella. Surely other men have wanted to kiss that gorgeous mouth. Contrary to what you might believe, I'm not a monster. I'm a decent man with a good heart, and many women would have loved to kiss me." He grinned, thinking he was being charming, then suddenly realizing once again that she couldn't *see* any of that charm. Damn!

"Let me out of this truck!" she yelled, straining against the seatbelt and pushing on the door. Poor Taco whined in the backseat, his cold nose laying against her neck. Razor looked at the woman beside him and smiled, her curves straining against the long-sleeved t-shirt, her black leggings making that beautiful ass look positively edible. She was a feisty one for sure. All that Latin temper wrapped in a body made for sin.

"Nope, and if you try to jump, you'll be dead in no time. I'm doing seventy-eight, and we're riding an edge of a cliff, so have fun flying."

"Ohhhh, you're so frustrating! I don't want my brother's criminal, drug-dealing, murdering friends helping me! Take me back to Atlanta," she yelled.

"Let's get something straight, Bella."

"Don't call me that!" She nearly shook with vehemence at his use of the shortening of her name. Tears welled in her eyes, and he almost complied. Almost, I mean, he was an asshole after all.

"Right, let's get something straight, Bella. I'm not one of your brothers' drug dealers, gang members, or even lackies. I'm not a fucking criminal. I met your brother while I was working as a therapist in the prison."

"A-a therapist," she repeated softly.

"That's right, sweetheart. It's not my full-time job. It was just temporary for a friend. My full-time job is designing and creating custom motorcycles and cars. I work for the Steel Patriots motorcycle club. I've never broken the law and don't intend to start now. I'm a retired Navy SEAL. I'm thirty-nine years old, never been married, no kids. I don't drink to speak of. I don't gamble, and I don't do drugs. If there's anything else you want to know, ask. But do not ever fucking call me a criminal or low-life again." He took a deep breath and continued.

"I am here to help you, to fulfill a promise I made to your brother after he helped me with something. So, I am going to keep that beautiful ass of yours safe."

She was quiet for several minutes, and he was grateful for the reprieve, if only for a few minutes. Her head angled slightly toward him, and she spoke.

"And what else would you like to do to my beautiful ass?"

CHAPTER EIGHT

Razor looked at the woman in the seat next to him and let out a long slow breath.

"I'll ask that again in a minute when you've had time to formulate your answer. You said you kissed me because you wanted to. You said you were certain other men wanted to kiss my pretty mouth. Why?"

"First of all, I said gorgeous mouth, not pretty. Second, why would you not think men wanted to kiss you? You're fucking stunning," he said, rubbing his forehead. He was getting a headache, and part of the reason was the woman sitting next to him making his cock rock-hard.

"I wouldn't know what men want, and I wouldn't know whether or not I'm fucking stunning. I have no idea if my mouth is gorgeous, or if I'm stunning, or ugly, or anything else," she said quietly. "The last time I saw myself in a mirror, I was eight years old. I could barely see it then, but I saw long brown hair, and I wore this lavender dress with sandals." Her voice sounded far away, and Razor swallowed, knowing she was reliving something she'd prefer not to.

"Hector, he was a good brother. He tried. I-I was so scared when I started to not be able to see. My parents wouldn't listen, and Hector, he took me to the eye doctor at the free clinic. The doctor said I had a degenerative eye disease. It was going to get worse, not better. I was too young to know what that meant, but Hector did."

"That must have been terrifying for both of you," said Razor, looking at the woman in the seat next to him. She nodded.

"Yes. My parents disappeared a few days later. They left a note for Hector telling him to take care of me. I was eight, and he was seventeen. How fair was that? His youth was stolen because now he had to take care of me. I know. I know what he did to get me into those schools. I know what he sacrificed. I don't agree with it, but I understand why he did it."

"We do a lot of shit for those we love, honey," said Razor. She turned slightly toward him at the sound of the endearment. "I didn't have siblings. Never met my parents. My abuela took care of me for as long as I can remember. She died when I was eighteen, but that death changed my life forever. I joined the Navy and met the brothers that I still work with today."

"Will you tell me about them? The Steel Patriots, you said, right?"

"Yea, Bella..."

"Please don't call me that," she whispered, a tear running down her cheek. He couldn't help himself as he lifted a hand and wiped the tear away.

"You're going to have to give me a reason, honey. Bella means beautiful, and from where I'm sitting, there's no other name to give you."

She continued to stroke Taco's big head, her fingers gripping his fur. He moaned and sensed her stress, sitting up, he nudged her face.

"It's okay, boy," she said softly. "That man, the one who attacked me, he called me Bella." Razor nodded.

"Well, he doesn't get to own that shit. You are fucking beautiful, honey. That's what I'm gonna call you, and know that it comes from a good place. Where was the dog during the attack?"

"He locked him in a closet. Poor Taco was trying to get out."

"Well, if he had, Baker might have hurt him, so I'm glad he was in that closet." She could only nod her head.

"Your friends?"

"Yea, well, we're all former military. Our team lead wanted us to continue to help where we could when we could. We all rode motorcycles while in the service and decided we would form a motorcycle club. Ghost, our lead, his pops left him a huge piece of land, and we converted the old barn into living quarters; the front of it is a bar and restaurant."

"You live in the bar?" she asked. He laughed and shook his head.

"No, Bella, the barn is separated by a steel wall. Between the restaurant and bar are two sets of steel doors. No one gets to the living space without the proper security. The garage, gym, and clinic are all on the property, but more toward the front with access to the main road. A lot of the guys have built houses on the property, so it's like we have our own private gated community."

"It sounds amazing," she said quietly. "Your friends... their names?"

"Ghost, he's married to Grace, and they have a little boy named JT. Whiskey is married to Kat; she's an attorney. Doc, our medic, is married to Bree, who is a counselor and therapist. Zulu is married to Gabrielle or Gabi. Most of us call her Angel eyes. She's got these almost glowing eyes. They're amazing." He winced at his words, but not seeing it bother Isabella, he continued.

"Gunner is married to Darby; she owns a bookstore in town. She has the cutest little girl, Calla. Gunner adopted her when they got married. Ace, Skull, Hawk, Eagle, Ice, and Axe are all single. Tango, one of my best friends, just got engaged to Taylor. She's the girl that's tied up in all this as well."

"How so?" she asked.

"Her stepbrother, he-he attacked her, sexually assaulted her when she was fourteen. He was cellmates with Gavin Baker, and they had the same tastes, shall we say. Somehow in all of this, he got Baker to agree to go after you if something happened to him. I don't know why or how. I just know that he won't stop. He's sick. It's how he's wired."

"I see. And this woman, Taylor? Is she still in danger?"

"She might be. We're not sure. Her brother died, as did her stepfather, who, as it turns out, was helping the stepbrother."

"Wow, that's quite a story," she said. "Wh-where will I be staying?"

"In the barn. The rooms are all suites, and you'll be in a room across from mine. I'll be close by, and believe me, no one can get in."

"You don't have your own home?" she asked.

"Haven't needed one," he said, grinning. "I've stayed in our guest cottage on occasion, but we try to leave that open for, well, guests who come to the property. Most would have to be someone we know and that has had a background check." He was babbling, and he knew it.

"It's tough for Special Forces when they retire. We're used to being in a team, being with our brothers. When we're suddenly thrust out there on our own, sometimes we have trouble. It's one of the reasons that the suicide rate for veterans is so high. Many have trouble acclimating to life after service. I've been lucky to have the guys with me, near me."

"You have a sadness in your voice. Why?"

Fuck, she was perceptive. He was hiding the sadness in his voice. That shit at the prison would not let him go.

"Lots of shit to be sad about, Bella. I'm all good, though, don't worry, just tired." He watched her from the corner of his eye, her hair pulled to one side now, the dark brown tresses so silky, showing the smooth skin of her long neck. He wanted to run his hands through that hair, grip it in one fist, and feel her naked flesh against his own.

Shit, you need to get laid.

"What do I look like?" she asked quietly.

"What?"

"What do I look like?"

"Y-you don't know what you look like?" She shook her head.

"I don't see anything, Razor, nothing. Sometimes vague shapes or shadows. I can touch my body and feel, but that's different. Unlike people who are born blind, I remember colors and shapes. I understand what that means." He nodded.

"Right, well, you're beautiful." She laughed a deep, sexy, throaty laugh.

"Razor, that doesn't tell me anything. What. Do. I. Look. Like?"

He was trying to gather his thoughts. Trying to find the right words to describe her without sounding like a fucking pervert.

"You have long, dark brown hair. It reminds me of the color of a light blend coffee, not too dark, not too light, just perfect. Your eyes are big and brown, little, tiny flecks of gold in them, and you have long thick black lashes. Your nose is perfect for your face. It has a small little curve to it." She laughed.

"I broke it two years ago," she said.

"You what?"

"I broke it. Ran into a wall, hard. Hazards of my illness. Believe me, I stumble and fall a lot, especially in a new place, so I hope you don't have anything too valuable laying around. Go on."

"Okay, your skin is the color of caramel, light and golden. Your legs are shapely, your thighs full, but you can tell that's from walking or taking the stairs a lot." She nodded, grinning. "Your..."

He shifted in his seat, adjusting his pants. His cock was pressed against his zipper so hard he would have a permanent indentation of the teeth if he didn't move it aside.

"Go on."

"Your waist is tapered in from your hips, which are perfectly curved. Your breasts are beautiful, honey. They're big and round, perfect for your body."

"You like my body?" she asked with a small grin, her head tilted to the side.

"Yea, a little too much," he said under his breath.

"How can you like it too much? You said you were single, right?"

"Yea, I'm single, but I'm supposed to protect you, not seduce you, honey. Besides, I can't take advantage..."

"Take advantage of the blind girl? Is that what you're thinking? Listen to me, Razor. I'm not stupid, and I'm not a virgin if that's what you're worried about. I've had sex, not a lot. Probably not as much as you, but I've had it."

"You've had 'it'?" he laughed. "Honey, just you calling sex 'it' tells me all I need to know."

"Oh? And what is that?"

"That when, and believe me, honey, it will be when we make love, you will never again call making love 'it'."

CHAPTER NINE

Razor pulled into the gas station to fill up and helped Isabella from the truck, Taco, of course, right on her heels. She stretched, and lord help him, those beautiful breasts were pressed against her t-shirt for him to drool over, the cold breeze making her big, perfect nipples stand at attention through the thin fabric.

"Are you hungry?" he asked, trying to distract himself.

"I could eat," she said.

"We'll go next door when I'm done. There's a little steak house where we can eat, and then we'll get back on the road." She nodded as she heard the ticking of the gas pump.

"Tell me what you look like, Razor."

"Me? I don't know. I'm six-foot-one, a hundred and ninety pounds or so. I have black hair, brown eyes. That's about it."

"That's not it. You described my legs, my hips, my chest. Tell me about your body." He looked around the gas pumps seeing that no one else was within earshot.

"Okay, I have a good bit of muscle definition because I work out regularly. I run, but my work also is very physical. My stomach is flat. My chest is wide, but not overly so. I have lean arms with good muscle definition. What else?" he asked.

"How big is your cock?" He nearly choked on his own saliva. Her face was as serious as anyone he'd ever spoken to.

"Wh-what?"

"You heard me. I just want to know."

"Why do you want to know?"

"I guess for reference. I mean, in movies and books that's all people talk about is the 'size of his package' or 'he was thick and long.' I'm trying to understand what that means." He looked at her face and realized she was serious.

"Come here," he said in a husky voice. She stayed where she was, and he said it again. "Come here, Bella."

Isabella moved toward his voice, reaching for his free hand. He pulled her body against his, grinding his hips into her belly, then reaching for her hand, he lay it against his length, wrapping her fingers around his jean-clad cock.

"That's how big I am, Bella. That's what I am dying to share with you." Isabella swallowed, her fingers gripped around his length. She rubbed the heel of her hand against him. "Bella," he swallowed.

"I-I like the feel of it," she whispered against his cheek. Razor cursed himself, grazing her jaw with his lips, working them around until they rested against her own. That feeling again. The warmth, the taste, those sweet plump juicy lips were like heaven for Razor.

He let his free hand pull her closer, and those lusciously full breasts smashed against his chest. He could feel the hard nipples poking through the fabric. Sliding his tongue into her mouth, he danced with hers, the heat penetrating his body. A horn sounded in the distance, breaking the kiss.

"Fucking hell, Bella, that was hot, baby," he said against her lips.

"Yea, yea, that was..." she was flushed the prettiest shade of pink, and he loved that he put that look on her face.

"Your cheeks are pink, Bella. I love that I did that to you." He kissed her again. "Did you get your answer?"

"Yes, approximately eight and a half inches and a good two to three inches in girth. You're a big boy." She moved around his body and stepped back into the truck, leaving him standing in the cold wind, praying

his cock would go down.

CHAPTER TEN

Isabella fell asleep about thirty minutes after leaving the restaurant. Razor was glad. He needed some time to think about what in the hell he was doing. Since the moment he'd met her, he was thinking with his dick instead of his brain. She was making him crazy!

He'd made a promise to Hector, and he was going to keep it, but what he hadn't planned on was keeping Isabella. Right now, that was exactly his fucking plan. He didn't think he'd be able to let her go. Not now, not ever. When he saw her in that motel room, he nearly had a heart attack. She was so damn beautiful, and the best part was, she had no clue. She was a natural beauty with curves earned from genetics, not plastic.

When she'd placed her hand on his cock and wrapped her fingers around him, he thought he would blow in his jeans. Just the nearness of her body, the sight of her breasts straining against the fabric, moving up and down with every breath, nearly sent him over the edge. She said she'd had sex, but damned if he would believe her. Or, if she had, it was a shitty experience.

Taco had his head lying between the opening of their seats, his nose never far from her hand. It was interesting to watch him protect her and guide her. His instincts were good, and more importantly, there was a love for his owner, which told Razor that she was good to the dog.

Now resting on his head was the thought of how he'd tell Hector about him and his sister. I mean, the guy was in prison, so there was that, but he wanted him to know that none of that was planned. Fuck!

Seeing the exit for their small town, he slowed, taking the curve, and felt the truck jerk to the left. At the same time, he heard a loud pop. Shit! He had a blowout. What the fuck? The tires were brand new, and there didn't appear to be anything on the road. Pulling over, he looked at Isabella's still sleeping form. The dog seemed to have sensed something was wrong but not her.

"Shit!" he murmured under his breath. It was pitch black outside, and he needed to change the damn tire. Finally, reaching in his pocket, he fished out his phone and dialed Ghost.

"You okay?" he said, picking up.

"Yea, brother, I'm at the exit near Main Street. Truck blew a tire." Glass shattered in every direction as Razor ducked, pulling Isabella with him. "Shots fired. Shots fired!" He heard Ghost scream 'fuck' and then knew he would be at their location soon.

"Bella, Bella, baby, we gotta get out," he said, pulling her with him. The bullet had come through on his side of the windshield, so the shooter was mostly likely directly ahead of them. If he could move her out on her side, he would get them to the buildings on Main and find a place to lay low.

"Wh-what happened?" she asked.

"We blew a tire, or someone blew it for us and then shot at us," he said, gripping her elbow as they moved around the truck. Using the darkness, he moved carefully to walk toward the alley behind Taylor's old coffee shop. Taco was right next to Isabella, comforting her with his cold nose. The wind picked up, and Razor felt a shiver run through Isabella's body. Pulling off his sweatshirt, he pulled it over her head.

"N-no, you'll get c-cold," she shivered.

"Doesn't matter, baby. You need to stay warm. Stay close to me, yea? Hold onto my belt. Here," he said, gripping her hand and guiding it to his waist. "Stay in step with me. Can you do that, Bella?"

"Y-yes," she said. He moved quickly behind the buildings and then ducked behind the dumpster behind the bookstore, shooting a text to Ghost.

"You did good, honey," he said quietly.

"Darkness is kind of my friend," she said, grinning. He kissed her nose and felt her warm breath exhale against his face. "I-I like when you do that."

"Do what, Bella?" he asked quietly.

"K-kiss me." He felt his phone vibrate and looked down to see the text he was waiting for. Ghost and the team were sixty seconds away. As he was about to stand, he felt Isabella's grip on his hand and looked down, then realized she was hearing what he now heard. Someone was in the alley, crunching against the glass and gravel.

Before he could figure out who or what it was, the sounds of trucks racing down the alley caught his attention. Three vehicles stopped directly in front of them, but the fourth continued down the alleyway.

"Gunner saw someone taking off. He's following," said Zulu. "Hello, beautiful. I'm Zulu."

"H-hello, I-I'm Isab-bella, and this is T-Taco," she shivered.

"Come on, honey. Let's get you in the truck." Razor set her and Taco in Zulu's truck, and then he walked back to the men. Ghost turned to him.

"What the fuck happened?"

"Came off the exit onto Main, and I thought my truck blew a tire. Now I think the fucker shot it out. Next thing I knew, he shot through the windshield while I was talking to you. Missed my head by an inch or so. He's a damn good shot."

"You're fucking lucky he wasn't better," said Ghost with a growl. "How's the girl?"

"Confused, scared."

"Let's get back. We can't do anything else out here tonight."

"Not leaving my truck, Ghost." He looked at him like he'd lost his mind.

"Of course, you're not, asshole, but we're all going to help change the tire and then follow you back." Twenty minutes later, the tire was changed, and they were pulling into the compound. Isabella was finally warmed from the heat of the truck, but now she had to step outside again. Her feet hit the soft earth and knew that it had rained here.

"It rained today?" she asked to no one in particular.

"It did," said Zulu.

"You should be able to find his footprints," she said thoughtfully. Zulu raised a brow at the woman and nodded, then realizing she couldn't see it, he spoke.

"That's true, and we'll send some boys back out to look for that. In the meantime, let's get you inside. George has got some hot food for you, and you can meet the girls." She nodded, taking his elbow as he led her inside. She felt his big warm fingers cover her own and took a mental note that this man was probably much bigger than Razor.

"Wh-where is Razor?" she asked.

"Right here, honey," he said, taking her elbow from Zulu. "Sorry, I was getting your bag." Opening the doors to the restaurant, they walked inside to find all the girls at one table, patiently waiting for the newcomer. Grace was the first to rise and greet her.

"Hello, Isabella," she said, extending her hand, sliding it gently into Isabella's, and pulling her closer to hug her. "I'm Grace. I'm married to that grouchy old guy, Ghost. Welcome to our home."

"Thank you so much," she said, smiling.

"Hello, Isabella. I'm Taylor. I'm afraid you and I are meeting under the worst possible circumstances."

"You're the woman, the other woman, he's threatening," she said with a tone of recognition and understanding.

"Yep, that's me, the lucky girl."

"Hi, Isabella. I'm Aubrey, but everyone calls me Bree."

"The counselor," she smiled.

"Yes indeed," laughed Bree.

"Hi, Isabella. I'm Kat, and this is Gabi."

"Hi, Isabella," said Gabi.

"Let's see, lawyer, doctor and Angel eyes," she laughed.

"Honey, you're gonna fit right in," said Gabi. "Darby is at home with Calla, who has a stomach bug. We'll meet up with her tomorrow, but if you need anything at all, let us know. Were you able to grab clothes, toiletries when you left?"

"I have a few clothes and just the basic toiletries. I don't use makeup. I mean, if I can't see it to enjoy it, why should anyone else," she smiled. There was laughter filled with tension, and Isabella raised her hands. "Sorry, I tend to use blind humor a lot. Just laugh with me. It will be easier."

"Are you hungry, honey?" asked a male voice. She turned to hear the new person and liked the sound of his voice. He was older; she knew that, but there was kindness and protection layered in his voice. "Sorry, I'm George."

"Hello, George, and yes, I'm starving actually," she said, smiling. "Is there any way I can get something for Taco? He needs a bowl of water, and his dog food, I think, is in the truck."

"Got it right here, gorgeous," said another new voice.

"Hawk? You wanna keep those pearly white teeth you'll back away from Isabella," said Razor. Hawk chuckled, and Isabella liked the sound of the man's laughter.

"Hawk, I'm Isabella. Thank you for bringing in the dog food."

"Any time, gor... Isabella," he laughed. "You need anything else, just let me know as long as your watchdog doesn't bite me."

"Oh, Taco doesn't bite," she said innocently.

"Not the dog I was talking about," said Hawk, laughing.

"Come on, Bella, let's sit and have some dinner, and then I can get you to the room," said Razor. She nodded, taking his elbow once again, but she paused as if unsure of where to step.

"Can you just, ummm, tell me the layout of the room," she asked no one in particular.

"Sure, honey," said Ghost. "How does it work best for you?"

"I can help," said Ace, coming toward her. "Hi, Isabella, I'm Ace, Alex Mills, but they call me Ace. You are about twenty feet inside the front doors. The room is a square, approximately two hundred and seventy feet across and two hundred and ninety feet long. There are twelve six-foot round tables situated at one, three, five, seven, nine, and eleven, and then moving inward in the same position about twelve feet away from the first circle. On the right wall is the bar. It's fifteen feet long with eight stools around it.

"Directly in front of you, if you walked about one hundred feet, is the first of our steel doors. Razor will make sure you have the codes, but the easiest thing for you will be handprint. All the hallways are eight feet wide, so there's plenty of space to move. Your room has been set up in a similar fashion, but again, Razor can show you that."

"Here is a phone with braille keys," he said, setting the phone in her hand. She noticed he held out her hand and almost dropped it in her palm. "You can activate it by voice. Keep it on you at all times, but there is a tracking device in it should anything happen. I've attached a small tracking chip to Taco's collar, and this is a bracelet for you." He fastened the bracelet around her wrist and then let out a long breath.

"I think that's it, but if you need anything else, I'm the first door through the second steel door." She heard him walking away and opened her mouth to speak, then heard the soft chuckles.

"What did I miss?" she asked.

"Honey, that was classic Ace. Welcome to the Steel Patriots."

CHAPTER ELEVEN

It was nearly midnight by the time Razor got Isabella to her room and settled inside. He made sure she was comfortable with the layout, only moving one item that she thought might cause her trouble. He also made sure she knew how to get across the hall to his room, then handed her the key.

"I'm a step away, but you can always call me too, honey," he said, kissing her forehead.

"Y-you could stay... here... with me."

"Bella? Are you scared, baby?" he asked, brushing her hair from her face.

"I-I'm not scared. It's just a new place, that's all. I'll be fine, Razor. I'm sorry I asked," she said, waving her hand in front of her. "I have Taco, and he'll be good company for me."

"Baby, listen to me. I want to stay, Bella. You know I do. You felt how much I do. I just think I should give you a little space to be sure."

"Are you giving me space to think, or you space to think, Razor?" she asked, tilting her head. Razor started to say something and then thought better of it. He gripped the back of her neck, pulling her toward him as he stepped forward into her body.

"I will have you in my bed, Bella. Have no doubt about that, but I want to be sure it's not because of all this craziness. I want you in my bed because you want to be there, not because you're scared, or not because you want to know what lovemaking feels like for the first time."

She opened her mouth and then closed it.

"H-how did you know?"

"Honey, you ooze inexperience, but it's fucking hot as shit. I will have you, Bella," he said, kissing her jaw, "all of you... every... square inch." His mouth trailed from her jaw to her ear lobe, then her cheek, and finally, he was attached to her lips once more.

Bella let out a small gasp and then moaned against his lips, her body pressed tightly against him. She felt that beautiful eight and a half inches again, the thickness of it making her wet.

"Sleep, Bella," he said, pulling away. "I'm across the hall if you need me." She nodded as he left and closed the door. Taco nudged her hand, and she rubbed his head.

"I know, boy. I tried." The room was small enough it was easy for Bella to make her way around the space, easily finding the shower. With her hair washed, she combed it out and braided it down her back, then pulled on the big sleep shirt she usually slept in. As she slid between the sheets, her thoughts went to the man across the hall.

Somehow, he knew she was bluffing about having sex before, and she was embarrassed by that. What twenty-eight-year-old woman was still a virgin? A blind one with a gang-leading brother, that's who. Remembering the feel of Razor's hands on her, his lips touching her own, she slid her hand between her legs and felt the wetness.

This was not going to do at all. Standing, she listened at the door for any noise and then slowly opened the door. Taking the four steps across the hall, she found the doorknob and opened it, closing it behind her.

"Bella? You okay, baby?" he asked. She shook her head, moving toward the sound of his voice. She heard him slide over in the bed, patting the mattress. "Lie down. Sleep."

Isabella lay against the warmth of the sheets, his body heat and scent still lingering. Reaching for his hand, she pulled it toward her body, laying it against her thigh and then silently guiding it up until his hand was lying against her soft, wet curls.

"Be sure, Bella. I don't take this lightly. We do this, you're mine, honey," he growled against her ear.

"I-I'm sure. I've never been surer. I want you. I need you," she whispered. Razor kissed her, leaning against her body. Pulling on the t-shirt, pulling it over her head, those beautiful breasts with the dark round nipples staring back at him, and he sucked in a gasp.

"You're fucking beautiful, Bella. Your body is gorgeous."

"T-touch me, please," she begged.

"Gladly, Bella." He shoved her knees apart and let his hands glide up her thighs, feeling the heat coming from her, all that heat waiting for him. "Can you smell it, Bella? Do you smell your desire?"

"Yes, yes, it's because of you. I've never smelled that before, felt the heat and wetness. My whole body is aching for you," she said quietly.

"Yea, baby, it is. I'm gonna put my fingers in that sweet pussy, Bella. I'm gonna make you come all over them, and then I'm gonna lick you clean, honey. All I'm doing is getting that perfect body ready for me." She nodded as she felt his fingers touch her opening, one long finger gliding down between her soft folds. She arched her back with a gasp of desire, and he smiled, watching those features fill with need.

Razor let his one finger slip inside her, turning it, rotating, and wiggling. She was so responsive, so needy for his touch. He pulled out and then slid two fingers in. Leaning forward, he plucked at one of her nipples with his teeth, and she exhaled. Taking that big breast in his free hand, he squeezed and lapped at the sweet brown nipple.

Isabella needed to feel him, needed to feel his body. Her hands found his arms, gliding up and then down his chest. He was smooth, no chest hair, and when her fingers glided over his stomach, she felt the rippling of muscle, and her nipples hardened even more. Letting her hand continue downward, she found his coarse black curls and then that beautiful long piece of desire.

Wrapping her fingers around him, she relished the feel of the velvety soft skin, the gentle weeping of liquid coming from the head as she wiped her thumb over the top of the hard length.

"Bella," he growled, "baby, I won't make it if you keep touching me like that."

"Then take me, for God's sake!" she begged. Razor chuckled, moving his fingers faster, scissoring inside her sweet tight pussy.

"That's it, baby. Let go for me," he said as her body shook with satisfaction. He pulled his fingers from her, taking them inside his mouth and tasting her. "You taste wonderful, Bella."

"I-I do?" she asked.

"Let me show you." Razor lowered his head between her legs, and she gasped as his tongue flicked against her sensitive skin. She felt him sucking and licking, and she desperately needed to feel more of him. He lifted his head, and she knew he was crawling toward her. Placing his mouth against hers, she tasted the salty flavor of her own desire. Sucking on his tongue, she found she liked the taste, then licked his lips.

"Yea, baby, you like that, don't you?" he growled.

"Yes, please..."

"I'll try to be gentle, honey. Let me do this." She nodded and spread her legs wider, offering his hips plenty of room. Razor let his big purple head touch her pink opening, and he moaned. Damn, he wanted to just drill his cock into her but knew he needed to do this easy. Pushing in just an inch or two at a time, he loved watching her face, the expressions of need, desire, wonder, and pain.

"Oh, R-Razor…"

"Diego, I'm Diego in our bed, baby," he said in her ear. "I'm making you mine, Bella, mine." With the last word, he covered her mouth and drove his cock inside her, feeling her barrier break, he knew she was probably hurting; he didn't want to be a bastard, but fuck, he needed to move inside this woman.

He stilled, kissing her sweetly, rubbing her sensitive nipples to distract her. When she started to instinctively move her hips against him, he took that as the okay. Rolling his hips into her full thick body, he felt that tight pussy squeezing his cock.

"You're-you're so big. Are all men this big?" she asked. He gave a quiet laugh, kissing her again.

"I'm better than average, honey, but a little tip, don't mention another man's dick while I'm inside you."

"S-sorry, oh, wow, Diego, whatever you're doing, keep, oh…"

"Yea, Bella, feel it, baby. Let go, honey. Let go and cum all over my cock." Razor pumped furiously inside her warmth, the feeling of her walls contracting around him, draining his cock of the buildup he'd been accumulating since he'd first seen her. He was gasping for air when they were done. Then he knew the mistake he'd made.

"Fuck, we didn't use protection, Bella. I'm sorry, honey. That's my fault."

"It's okay. I mean, I can get the morning after pill or something," she said calmly. Razor nodded but wasn't sure he liked that idea at all. If they'd made a baby together, he was going to be fucking thrilled about it. Hector probably not so much.

"Let's not worry about it tonight, honey. Let me clean you up, and we'll sleep." By the time he'd wiped the evidence of their lovemaking from her body, she was softly snoring. Razor smiled, thinking it was the cutest damn thing he'd ever seen. He heard a chuff at the door and opened it quickly, only to find Taco waiting patiently.

"Thanks for waiting for the grand finale, buddy," he said, rubbing his head. "Come on in. You and me gotta protect her, right?" Taco looked up at Razor and whined.

"Yea, I'm talking to dogs now. I'm perfectly sane."

CHAPTER TWELVE

Three days later, Razor walked back from the shop to have lunch with Bella. Not seeing her in the restaurant, he jogged up the stairs, stopping outside their room. He heard soft voices. Leaning closer to the door, he realized she must be watching a movie. What he heard, though, was hard to believe.

She threw her leg over his thick steel rod, lowering her sweet cunt onto him. She sighed 'sounds of sighing' and gripped his head, pulling him toward her breast. 'Suck my tits,' she told him. Suck them, and then if you're a good boy, I'll suck you.'

What in the holy fuck was she listening to? He opened the door, and Bella gasped.

"What are you doin', Bella?" he asked, grinning at her.

"Oh, ummm, did you hear that?" she said, blushing.

"Baby, I couldn't help but hear that, and now, I'm rock hard for you," he said, sitting next to her. "What is that?"

"Well, the girls, Grace and everyone, they're reading these books, and they wanted me to catch up so I could have book discussions with them, and well, they're really interesting and informative, and since I don't have much experience and these books have lots of sex in them they thought maybe I should listen to them because they don't come in braille, but maybe I need to get headphones." She finally stopped, taking in a deep breath, and Razor pulled her to him.

"I'll tell you what, sweet girl. Why don't you and I listen to those books together," he said.

"Wh-what? R-really? You would do that?" she said, snuggling into him.

"I would so do that, baby. That was fucking hot as shit, and I want to experiment and do all the things those naughty books tell you to do," he said, pulling her in for a kiss. "Come on, I thought we'd have lunch, and then I have to get back to the shop."

She gripped his elbow as Taco followed them downstairs. At the bottom of the steps, Ace stepped out of his office.

"Hi, Isabella," he said, nervously looking from her to Razor.

"Hi, Ace. How are you?"

"Uh, I'm good. Listen, I should have warned you that I can oversee and hear all communication on the electronic devices. Sooo, maybe when you're listening to the audiobook, you put your privacy settings on, k?"

"Oh God," she whispered. Razor chuckled next to her, and she elbowed him. "It's not funny! I'm so sorry, Ace. Did I embarrass you?"

"No, no, not at all, I learned a few things," he said, grimacing as he looked at Razor.

"Privacy settings, got it," she said, walking through the steel door.

Razor pulled her toward the table with the others while George brought out hot stew and sandwiches. Taco settled next to her as they enjoyed their lunch. She felt him suddenly sit up, and then a low growl emanated from his throat.

"Taco? What's wrong, baby?" she asked, rubbing his head. The dog started barking, and Razor turned, placing his body between hers and the door. Tango stepped in front of Taylor, Ghost pushing Grace behind him.

Taco was going crazy, growling and barking at the front doors.

"Let him go," said Isabella. "Go, Taco, find." The dog took off toward the front door, pushing the big doors open and running.

"Follow the dog!" yelled Zulu to Hawk and Eagle.

The two young men took off running behind the door, stepping out into the cold autumn wind. The parking lot was filled with lunchtime crowd patrons, and they scanned the area. Taco was running from car to car, eventually stopping beside one and barking. Eagle ran to the door of the vehicle, ready to open it to someone hiding, when he saw the tripwire.

"Get back!" he yelled. "Taco, back, boy, back!"

Hawk pushed back and then through the doors. Eagle followed with Taco.

"Get the women secure," he said to Ghost. Eagle was not usually the loud, give orders kind of guy. His twin damn sure was, but he was usually the strong silent type. Right now, he was anything but silent. "There's a car in the parking lot rigged with about a hundred pounds of C4. Get them out of the barn. Get the regular customers across the field and into the garage. I'm going to see if I can cut the wires."

"NO!" yelled Ghost. "Don't fucking touch it. We'll call the bomb squad guys." Eagle shook his head.

"It'll be too late. There's a timer. Go," he said, running toward the door.

"Eagle!" yelled his brother. Looking back at his teammates and friends, he smiled. "He's my twin, man. Gotta go."

"Fuck!" yelled Razor. "Let's go. Get them locked down. Zulu, Gunner, and Ghost stay with them. I'll see if I can help the boys."

"Diego," he heard the soft cry of Isabella.

"It's okay, Bella, go with them," he kissed her forehead. "I'll be back, baby."

Razor took off through the front door while the others ushered the customers and the women to a secure location. He took note of the car that was rigged, parked next to his truck. Fucker planned this, hoping he would either kill Razor, or him and Bella together.

"Hawk? You get your ass killed, I'm going to be fucking pissed at you, brother," said Razor, standing in the distance.

"Not as pissed as I'll be," he grinned. "Simple wiring, very basic, snip the door," he said, carefully opening the door and cutting the wire. He looked under the seat, no pressure trigger. "Okay, timer. We got this. We got this."

"Timer is moving fast," said Eagle.

"I know. You telling me the obvious doesn't help." Hawk saw and knew there was nothing to do. "Uh, Razor, how much do you love your truck?"

"Why?"

"Fucking run!"

Hawk and Eagle took off toward Razor, standing at the door. They felt the rumble and then the pressure from the blast lifting their bodies, slamming them against the barn. Eagle's big body hit Razor, his arms wrapping around the younger man, trying to protect him from the blow. Debris flew in the air, metal, tires, and glass.

When the ringing in his ears finally stopped, Razor looked down at Eagle, his nose bleeding, a few cuts from glass on his face.

"You okay?" he asked. Eagle looked up, squinting. "Are you okay?" he yelled. Eagle nodded. As Razor lay him down against the door, he ran toward Hawk's body lying face down in the mud. Gently rolling him over, he winced.

"Shit, shit, shit," he repeated. "Hawk? Brother, open your fucking eyes, Hawk!" he yelled.

"Stop fucking yelling," he moaned. Razor let out a long slow breath. "Guess your truck is toast, right?"

"Don't give a shit about my truck, brother. What the fuck happened?"

Ghost and Zulu came running towards them, Zulu leaning down next to Eagle, checking his pupils. Ghost ran to Razor and Hawk.

"What the fuck happened?"

"That's what I just asked," said Razor, grinning at the big man.

"Fucking car next to Razor's truck was loaded with C4. Thought it was an easy fix, rigged to a timer, but when I cut the tripwire on the door, it triggered a secondary timer, sped the fucker up. I had eight seconds. Eagle? Where the fuck is Eagle?"

"He's okay," said Razor, pushing him back down. "He's fine, just a little glass."

"How in the hell does this guy know how to rig C4 to tripwires and timers? First, he gets off a killer shot taking out your tire, then nearly hitting your head, and now this. This guy is not just some pervert from prison," said Ghost.

"We need to call Shred, and see what else he can tell us," said Razor. Ghost nodded, reaching into his pocket for his phone. He dialed Whitey and asked that Shred come up as soon as he was able.

By the time the fire department had come and gone, the customers left with damaged vehicles, and the police reports were made, the team was exhausted. Someone had gotten onto the property and come damned near close to killing them. He was not fucking happy.

Seated in Ghost's living room, the women were huddled close to each of their men, the men talking about what to do next.

"Isabella? How did Taco know what was going on?"

"He was originally a trained bomb and search and rescue dog, but something happened to make them not pass him through for final use. I was able to buy him, and he's been with me now for seven years. He's really special. Most guide dogs protect you somewhat, but Taco goes the extra mile. He not only guides me, but he protects me as well, and as you saw today, can sometimes detect dangers that other dogs may not."

"Obviously, Bella," said Razor, kissing her forehead. "That dog saved our asses today. Had he not alerted us that something was going on in the parking lot, people might have been killed." Bella stood and called for Taco.

"Where are you going, honey?" asked Zulu.

"I-I have to leave. You have children here. You're not safe because of me. You're not safe." She started to move toward the door, hitting her shin on the coffee table and falling forward. Gunner grabbed her as her body pitched forward, gently holding her in his arms and then setting her upright.

"Whoa, honey, you're not going anywhere," he said, turning her to face Razor.

"Razor, Diego, you have to... you have to let me go..."

"I don't have to do shit, baby. You're not leaving here. These homes are secure. This property is secure. What happened out in that parking lot was an anomaly. There is nowhere safer than right here, honey." She shook her head and felt the tears falling down her face.

"I can't let you all risk your lives for me."

"You don't have a choice, Isabella," said Ghost. "See, I'm the team lead here. I protect my men and by extension, protect their families. You, my sweet girl, are Razor's family. You aren't going anywhere, and we will make sure that everyone is safe."

"I don't understand why you would do this for me. I'm practically a stranger to all of you. I'm a liability. I'm what he wants. I can't even see to protect myself! I'm useless to all of you. You can't…" she yelled. Zulu stood and moved toward her, nodding at Razor. He lifted a big arm above her head, and she flinched, raising her arms to stop the blow she felt coming.

"Seems to me, pretty girl, that you can protect yourself. You might not have seen my big arm come up, but you damn sure felt it."

"Can you see shadows, Isabella?" asked Gabi.

"Some, it's better some days than others. Sometimes, I can see faint color and shadow, other days nothing."

"If you can see that," said Zulu, "I can teach you to defend yourself."

"Y-you can?"

"I can, beautiful," smiled Zulu. "Lessons start tomorrow."

She turned into the waiting arms of Razor and cried. When she had no more tears to shed, Grace led her into the kitchen with the other women, hoping to allow the men time to talk and plan.

"Can you really teach her to defend herself, Zulu?" asked Razor.

"Yep. She felt the air from my arm. She saw my shadow in front of her. I think she might see more than she thinks. We're gonna keep her safe, brother." Doc walked in, followed by Hawk and Eagle, cursing as he walked.

"Fucking hard-headed, twin stubborn fuckers," he growled.

"We love you too, Doc," said Hawk, grinning. Eagle, however, was not grinning at his brother. Hawk looked at him. "What?"

"You're an idiot. I told you to wait. I asked you not to open that door. You and your damned hero complex. Fucking asshole nearly died, and you think it's funny." Eagle never spoke more than a few words at a time. His brother knew he'd struck a chord with him.

"I'm sorry. You're right, Eagle. I'm sorry. I-I remembered a car like that in Islamabad. I was certain it was exactly the same."

"Well, it wasn't," said Eagle, slouching on the floor. His brother slid down the wall and gripped his knee, giving it a brotherly love squeeze.

"I know. I'm sorry." Eagle nodded, leaning his head back against the wall.

"You think you saw this exact thing before?" asked Razor, eyeing Hawk.

"Identical, I'm positive, brother. I know explosives, and this was exactly what we saw in Islamabad."

Razor nodded, looking at Ghost.

"Did Shred mention if his brother had military experience? Police? Anything?"

"No, nothing. But we're damn sure gonna find out. Ace?" he called across the room to the man sitting at the bar with his laptop. "See what you can find on Gavin Baker. I'm wondering if he's a blood brother or adopted. Maybe he's older than we thought. I don't think I ever asked how old he was." Ace simply nodded and began pecking away on the computer.

"I think I want us to stick close, groups. Zulu, Gabi, and the boys stay here. Gunner, Darby, Calla, Tango, and Taylor together. The rest of you pair up or triple up. No one is alone in the houses." Ghost stood walking around, running his hands through his hair. "Fuck, I wish we had bigger fences."

"Well, they're not bigger," said Ace, raising his finger and hitting a key on his keyboard, "but as of right now, they're electrified. One touch will kill anyone or anything. He won't get over the fences."

"Jesus, I love you," said Razor, smiling at him. He looked appalled at first and then grinned.

"I like you a lot too."

CHAPTER THIRTEEN

Seated around the breakfast table were every member of the Steel Patriots, their wives, girlfriends, and the staff. Whitey, Shred, and Crash walked in shortly after they all took their seats, looking refreshed from their long drive. Ace was in his customary seat at the counter within listening distance but still far enough away that he didn't worry about feeling crowded. He glanced quickly at Isabella and felt himself blush.

He didn't mean to listen in on the audiobook that Isabella was listening to the other night. His ears were trained to hear when things weren't quite right, and the voice on the audiobook was not someone he'd ever heard before. He routinely scanned the electronic devices to check for anyone who might be listening in. He never intended to hear the erotic story. The problem was once he started listening, he had a hard time turning it off.

Unlike his brothers, his experience with women was practically zero. The few girlfriends he'd had were told right away about his intimacy issues and said they were fine with it. As the relationships went on, when they wanted sex, he knew he'd have to warm up to it and suggested watching one another get off by their own hand. Two were fine with that for a few weeks and then had enough. One flat-out called him a freak.

After that experience, he'd pretty much resolved to taking care of his issues by his own hand. But that audiobook opened his mind to new possibilities and definitely some very hot thoughts. For now, he was more concerned with keeping his team safe.

"Boys," said Ghost, staring at the three men, "welcome back. Get yerselves some breakfast."

"I'm sure sorry about all this, Ghost," said Shred, shrugging his shoulders.

"Not your fault, man. We just need more information about your brother. Should have done it last time, but let's figure this out. Start at the beginning."

"Okay, Gavin was a late baby for my parents."

"Wait? He's not older than you?" asked Razor, looking confused.

"No, he's ten years younger."

"How can that be? I was told he served twenty."

"He was sentenced to twenty. The girl he was convicted of assaulting and raping was seventeen. She came forward about two years ago and said it was consensual, and they should release him. We all knew it was a lie, but she insisted. Gavin was twenty-one when he was convicted. He was on leave from the Army."

"Oh fuck," groaned Hawk, running his fingers through his thick, dark blonde hair.

"What? What did I miss?" asked Shred.

"How old is your brother now?" asked Hawk.

"Twenty-eight. He served seven, and when she came forward, he got it reduced to time served. Shit of it is, she was killed three weeks ago. Alleged hit and run."

"Damn, you can't be serious?" said Ghost. Shred shook his head.

"Where was your brother stationed?" asked Hawk.

"Middle East is all I know. As I said, we didn't talk much. I never understood how he even got into the Army. I mean, he is fucked up. I thought they did psyche evaluations and that shit. No way he was able to pass that shit as far as I can tell. I'm pretty sure the guy was screwing with explosives and shit."

"Ace? Pull his…"

"Got 'em," he said, turning to speak to everyone. Razor smirked at him. "What? Anyway, he was stationed with the 153rd out of…"

"Islamabad," said Eagle.

"Yea. He was written up on charges multiple times for taking a sympathetic stance against the enemy. He even participated in an anti-America protest in the main market square… in uniform."

"Christ, that sounds like my brother," said Shred.

"His CO began suspecting that he'd shot several of his own team but couldn't prove it. Pulled him from any details outside the wire. Ended up relegating him to a desk role until he went AWOL on…"

"September 27th," said Hawk. Ace looked up, frowning.

"You wanna read this?" he asked the other man.

"Sorry, brother, but September 27th was the day I disarmed the car in Islamabad. The same one that looked like the car in the lot the other day. That car belonged to one of the local tribal chiefs. He was attending peace talks with our military, the British, and their own military leaders. I was able to disarm the bomb, but two days later, another went off, killing the guy." Ace nodded his head.

"September 29th, he went AWOL again... was returned to base and sent home for a disciplinary hearing on October 1st. October 7th is when the attack and rape happened for Carrie Grisse, seventeen years old. She said she was walking home from a late swim practice for her high school when Gavin pulled over in his uniform and asked her if she needed a ride home. She accepted, thinking if he was in the military, it would be okay."

"Jesus, that kid trusted him because he was in uniform," said Zulu.

"Yea, she said he asked if she wanted to stop for something to eat, and she agreed. He seemed nice at first, then said they should get to know one another better. She woke up with him on top of her. She was naked; he was naked, and he was raping her. She didn't remember much after that. Authorities found several drugs in her system, most likely placed in her food."

"Damn," said Shred, looking as though he might cry.

"He's blood, man, but that don't mean it's your blood too," said Gunner.

"Go on, Ace," said Whiskey.

"Rape kit was performed and confirmed that she was raped. It was not consensual in any way, according to the hospital reports. She testified in court against him, to great detail about what happened, and he was sentenced to twenty years. As I said earlier, she showed up at his attorney's office a year and a half ago saying she wanted to retract her statement. Said she'd been confused and was sorry but that he deserved to be free."

"He was holding something over her... he... Louis Black. Louis Black was the only one who could get to her," said Razor. "He was out and free. He could have gotten to the girl at the request of his son."

"Shit!" yelled Ghost. "Ace? Was he trained in bomb disposal?"

"Some, he started the training and then was rejected for final entry due to 'erratic behavior.' Doesn't say what that behavior was. I can call Admiral Crossing and ask if he could find out." Ghost nodded.

"Yea, let that bastard start returning some favors. Shred? Where would your brother go? Was he an outdoor guy? Could he survive in the wilderness?"

"Not when I knew him," said Shred, shaking his head. "Dude liked his comforts. If I had to guess, he's hiding in plain sight. We look nothing alike, or we didn't last I saw him. He's a good three or four inches shorter than me, heavier around the middle, brown eyes, thinning brown hair."

"Any tattoos?" asked Whiskey.

"Again, none that I knew of last we saw one another." Ace stood and turned to the group.

"I just sent his prison release photo to your phones. Despite the fact that he was released early, he is still serving probation, which is why the BOLO and warrant are out on him. Although they threw out the charge of rape and assault, he still had sex with a minor, according to state laws. You're right. He looks nothing like you."

"I think I need to go visit with Castro," said Razor.

"No fucking way," said Whiskey. "That place nearly took your soul, brother. You're not going back in there."

"I'll be okay. I'll bring the twins with me and see if they can stay out of trouble," he said, grinning.

"I want to go," said Isabella.

"Sorry, Bella, your cute little ass is staying right here," said Razor.

"You can compliment my cute little ass some other time, Diego, but I'm going with you. I want to speak to my brother." Razor looked at his brothers in silence, each one giving a short nod. "If you think I can't hear your silent speak, you're wrong. Ghost? You let out a short, clipped sigh when you nod. Whiskey? Get your vertebrae checked – you crack every time you nod your head. Zulu? If you move a muscle, I smell your cologne. It's lovely, by the way. Gunner? Your nod is longer, and you tend to let a breath out between your lips. Doc? You lick your lips before you nod. Ace, you're very good."

"And me, princess?" asked Razor, grabbing her waist.

"I always know what you're thinking, mi amour." She practically purred her response, and Razor's dick jumped sky-high. Every man in the room felt his eyebrow raise.

"See, hide your emotions, gentlemen. A woman's voice shouldn't make everyone breathe heavier," she said, turning back to the table of women, all grinning at her.

"That woman's voice should," murmured Hawk.

"You wanna live another day, boy, you'll not look at my woman that way," growled Razor.

"Geez, once again, I may be a man-whore, but I don't sleep with my brothers' women! I do have some morals."

"Yet," said Eagle, smiling. "You haven't slept with a brother's woman yet." His twin couldn't help but grin at him as Razor kicked his boot.

"Get up, you shitheads," smiled Razor. "I guess we're taking a field trip to prison. Grab the big guns. I'll call the warden. Bella? Let's go, honey. Time to put on your loosest sweatshirt because you sure as shit are not walking in that prison looking like that." He stood, headed toward the door, and Isabella turned to the other women.

"What's wrong with the way I look?" she asked quietly.

"Not a damn thing, girl," laughed Gabi, "not a single damn thing."

CHAPTER FOURTEEN

Razor stood outside the main gate and let out a big sigh. He did not want to enter into this shithole again. He knew it was just as a visitor, but still, this shit was not okay. He looked at Isabella, her hair pulled back in a ponytail, his big Go Navy sweatshirt covering those perfect breasts. Hawk and Eagle were standing behind her, basically blocking an attack from the street.

Stepping through the gates, they were led to a private meeting room arranged by the warden. As he stepped through, Henry smiled at him.

"Dr. Diaz," he grinned, watching him walk toward him.

"Dr. Diaz?" said Isabella.

"Just a joke, honey. Henry, nice to see you, man. You doing okay?" asked Razor.

"Doing fine, Razor. Thanks for everything you did. My life has been infinitely better since your last visit." Razor nodded.

"Henry, this is Isabella Castro, Hector's sister."

"Well, it's a pleasure to meet you, Miss Isabella. Your brother is a decent enough fella," he said, grinning as he reached out his hand. When she didn't look down or take it, Razor gently pulled her hand forward, and Henry shook it. "Sorry about that, Miss Isabella. I didn't know."

"Don't be sorry, Henry. It's nice meeting you."

"Now, there's the prettiest sister known to mankind," said the familiar voice. "What the hell are you doing here?"

"Nice to see you again, Hector," smiled Razor.

"Why is my sister here?" he asked again.

"Speak to your sister," said Isabella. "I'm blind, not deaf, you asshole." Hector rolled his eyes and grinned at his sister.

"My hermana still has a mouth on her. Are you okay, Izzy? Has someone hurt you?" he asked.

"Someone tried, but Diego has been protecting me."

"Diego, is it?" grinned Hector.

"Uh, listen, Hector. Let's get this out of the way..."

"Do you remember when we first met, Razor?" asked Hector, eyeing the other man up and down. "You said to me that you had a weakness for full-bodied women with brains." Razor nodded, realization dawning on him.

"You knew," he grinned. "You bastard, you knew that if I met her, I would fall in love with her. Didn't you?"

"A brother knows these things. You looked like a good man. You're a stand-up, decent dude. You're not a criminal. You're smart. You're good-looking, and you're Latin," he grinned. "I wanted someone good for my sister. I wanted to know she was taken care of."

"You set us up!" she yelled.

"No, I just asked for a favor, and he agreed," said Hector. "I love you, Isabella, and in here, I can't be there for you anymore. It kills me a little more every day. When Razor and I helped each other out with something, I knew that if I asked him to protect you, he would. You know why? Because he's that kind of man. A man that any brother would be happy to give his sister to. I didn't know if you would fall in love, but I'm guessing by the way he's looking at you that he has fallen in love with you."

"I... wh-what?" she said. "H-have you? Are you?"

"Bella, baby, what do you think has been happening these last two weeks? Yes, I'm falling in love with you, baby." He leaned over and kissed her mouth, partly open in surprise.

"I-I love you too, Diego," she whispered.

"I know, baby, believe me, I know. Now, Hector, your sister wanted to see you, and I agreed only to make sure you understood that she's mine."

"Understand, and I'm happy, man, really," smiled Hector.

"Okay, now to business. Baker."

"What's the fucker done now?" Razor went through the events of the last few weeks, describing what had happened with Baker in Atlanta, the incident with the truck, and then the bomb in the car.

"My question is this, what could he possibly gain from hurting your sister? Black and his father are dead. He's out, free. What is there left?" Hector looked at Razor and then looked at his sister.

"Can... can she step out, please?" asked Hector.

"Hector, I love you. You're my brother..."

"I know, hermana, but some things you don't need to hear, please, my precious," he pleaded.

"It's okay, baby, step outside with Hawk and Eagle. Henry will entertain you." She nodded and took Hawk's arm. Eagle turned back.

"Sure you don't want me to stay?" he asked.

"Naw, man, we're good." He waited until the door clicked shut and turned back to Hector, chained on the other side of the table. "Okay, Baker."

"Yea, Baker. Listen, when I saw him come in his first day, I knew someone would make him their bitch quick. There was nothing attractive about the dude, so I passed. I did, however, give the okay for someone else to take him. Big fucker by the name of Tank. Let's just say he's not a very kind or caring lover."

"Fuck," growled Razor.

"Yea. When Baker found out it was me that gave him to Tank, he swore he'd get to me. Fucker didn't have the power to get at me inside, but he got to be friends with Black. Black told him about my sister. He's not doing this shit for Black; he's doing it to get even with me for giving him to Tank."

"So, he's pissed because he was made the bitch of some big dude?" said Razor.

"That's not all, brother. He... he was castrated by Tank with a very dull knife. Dude was in the prison hospital for three months recovering from that shit. He was fucked up before, but after, he was like Norman Bates crazy."

"Oh damn."

"It's my fault, Razor. My sister is in danger, again, because of me," he said, fighting the tears. Razor knew what it was costing this man to hold onto his emotions.

"Listen, brother, it's survival of the fittest in here. I'm not judging you. This fucker Tank, he still around?"

"Naw, got transferred to a maximum security two years ago. He was killed by another guy bigger than him. Can you protect her?"

"With my life," said Razor confidently. Castro nodded his head, biting his lower lip.

"Will you... will you send me wedding pictures?" he asked.

"You know I will, man. Course, I gotta convince her to marry my ass, and she is one stubborn woman," he grinned.

"Yea," laughed Castro, wiping his eyes, "she is that. Now she's your stubborn problem. Do me a favor, Razor?"

"Another one," he grinned. "Last one had me falling in love with your sister. What now?"

"Promise you'll love her forever."

"That's an easy promise, Hector. Easiest promise I'll ever make."

CHAPTER FIFTEEN

Gavin Baker watched the snow fall outside his motel room window. Snow. It was always so pure, white, giving a virginal look to the tainted earth after her evils and wrongdoings spilled out onto the dirt. As if cleansing it of all the sins from summer. He heard the soft moan behind him but ignored it.

Looking down at his hand, he hissed as he moved his fingers. His brother, his fucking older brother. When he saw him outside of Atlanta, it was as if the gift had been dropped in his lap. He started toward him without a second thought, forgetting how much bigger he was than him. He'd taken a swing at Gavin's head and connected but didn't see the glint of silver as it rammed into his side, tearing flesh and bone.

How could he betray him? His own flesh and blood testified against him during the trial. It wasn't like Shelby was their sister or something. She was their cousin. At only eleven, she was overly developed and definitely enjoyed showing it off, already a little tease just like her mother. Of course, no one knew that Aunt Terri was the one who showed him how to please a woman. It didn't matter. She'd been killed in a drunk driving accident, no loss to the earth. More snow needed for that one.

When he arrived home from the military, little Shelby had thrown herself into his arms, pressing those big, firm breasts against his chest, kissing his cheek. She knew what she was doing. She knew exactly what she was doing. He'd invited her to go for a hike, and she jumped at the chance; finding a secluded spot, he recommended they cool off with a dip in the lake; when she didn't want to get her clothes wet, he'd convinced her that swimming in her panties and bra was fine.

She watched him as he stripped off his clothes, his cock already hard; her cheeks turned pink, but her gaze never wavered, watching him walk into the water and soon followed. Those big breasts of hers bounced in the water, and when they started to play tag, he gripped one breast hard, and she yelped. She enjoyed it; he knew she enjoyed it.

As she tried to step from the water, he yanked on her panties, ripping them from her body. She had nowhere to go, nowhere to run. She tried to say she didn't want it. She tried to run, but he knew it was all part of the game. Yes, indeed, Gavin had one of the best afternoons of his life until she was found.

It wasn't his first time, but he'd made a crucial mistake by letting others see him walk off with her. It was sheer luck that she went catatonic. No way to prove it was him. Of course, the girl several days later turned out to be another issue. That bitch wanted it too. Yea, she was in sweatpants and a sweatshirt, but he could see the wet imprint of her high school swimsuit beneath the fabric.

When he started writing to her from prison, telling her how much he was in love with her, wanted a life with her, she'd bought into every word. Yep, smarter than every last bitch out there. He felt the twinge of an erection and then reached down to rub his cock, cringing.

It was like an amputee having phantom pains. There were times when he was certain it was still there, and other times like a few hours ago, when it was more than obvious. The woman lying tied to his bed almost burst out laughing when his little nub stared her in the face. She tried to get up and get dressed, but he made sure she had nowhere to run.

He'd strapped on a big dildo and taught her a few lessons about making fun of him. Now she was a bloody mess on his bed, and he'd have to get rid of her. He had time; she wasn't going anywhere.

Neither was Isabella Castro. Blind whore sister to Hector. He thought he ruled the cell block, but he had another think coming. He would teach him all about who Gavin Baker was and what he did to those who betrayed him.

His bigger issue now was all the men surrounding her. She seemed to have twenty-four-seven protection, and they were skilled. Not as good as he was, but still, they would make it challenging.

Blowing out the tire had been easy, then the windshield. He hadn't adjusted correctly for the wind, missing the driver by just inches. Then the lovely little surprise in the car. The twins who'd come out shocked him with their quick action and skill. They looked as though they knew what they were doing, and that was disappointing. Although, they didn't know enough. He smiled again, looking back at the woman lying on the bed.

"What do you say to round two, pet?"

CHAPTER SIXTEEN

"So, I think if we do the two turkeys, yams, mashed potatoes, asparagus, green beans, oyster dressing and the traditional bread dressing, homemade cranberry sauce, plus the rolls, that should be good for the meal," said Grace to the other women at the table.

"I can make an appetizer and my walnut fudge," said Isabella.

"Perfect, honey," said Grace. "Let us know what you need for us to buy and if you need any help in the kitchen. I know your place at home is probably perfect, but George has his kitchen a certain way."

"Don't you worry none about that, Isabella," said George. "You and I will get along just fine in the kitchen."

"Thank you, George," she smiled in his direction.

"I'll make the pies again," said Bree.

"I'm not a great cook," said Kat, "but I can make the centerpieces. I saw this super cute idea on Pinterest, and I've been dying to try it."

"I think we have it, ladies!" Grace smiled at the table, and the others clapped their hands.

"I do need some help with something," said Isabella.

"Anything, honey." Darby gripped her hand, smiling.

"When we left Atlanta, I left with only a few of my things. I desperately need clothing, and online shopping has never been very successful for me. If I tell you my sizes and give you my credit card, can you help me buy some things?"

"Oh, girl, you've come to the right place," smiled Kat. "Shopping is my middle name. Just ask my grumpy husband."

"Well, honestly, I wanted to do some shopping in CC Robat's recommended site for some lingerie," she blushed.

"Wait, our romance writer sells lingerie?" asked Grace. "I've never seen that in her books or his books? I mean, is CC a man or woman? It can't possibly be a man, right?" Isabella laughed, nodding.

"No clue, but maybe it's only in her audiobooks, but someone speaks about it at the end of every book I've listened to so far. The website claims to have all the items mentioned in the books – lingerie, leather, toys, everything. I'm serious. I want some of what she sells. I just need for all of you to look at it and tell me if you think it's worth it."

"What's the site?" asked Bree.

"tigressunleashed.com. According to the person who advertises it at the end, it's how she gets her inspiration for the books."

"It must be so different listening to the books than reading them," said Darby.

"Yea, I mean, I guess," said Isabella. "I've always either done braille or audiobook, so I really don't know the difference. The voices on the recordings are super sexy, so that helps."

"Oh, then I'm out," said Taylor. "When I read those books, the only voices I hear in my head are mine and Tango's. I don't want to be listening and suddenly hear another man, thinking that's the voice that's gonna do all those wonderful things to me."

Gabi and Darby laughed, shaking their heads.

"This last book, the one with the big ex-professional lineman – tall, chocolate, nothing but muscles. I'm telling you, girls. That's my man." Gabi grinned from ear to ear, winking at Zulu across the room.

"Holy shit," whispered Isabella. "If that's your man, you must not walk very well after a night alone." The laughter picked up again as Ghost, Whiskey, and Razor walked to the table.

"Are you ladies drinking tonight?" asked Whiskey. Kat stood and kissed him on the lips, gripping his ass cheek in her hand. She let her other hand dance down his arm, then, pulling his hand, she forced him to follow her toward the private rooms in the back. Whiskey's face was filled with shock but, more importantly, desire.

"What in the hell is going on here?" asked Ghost.

"Oh, honey, it's harmless. You know we have book club, and we just finished another book. Let's just say it reminded us of someone," she said, smiling. "Now, I'd like to see you in your office, alone."

"What the ever-loving fuck..." he growled.

"Are you actually going to question this?" said Razor. Ghost looked at his brother and shook his head. Was he stupid or something? Of course, he wasn't going to question it. He disappeared toward his office with Grace.

"How are you, baby?" asked Razor, looking at the table of women, all grinning in his direction.

"I'm good, Razor. I just need to do some online shopping with the girls, and then I'll be ready to head upstairs."

"Okay, anything I can help with?" he asked.

"NO!" came the loud cries of all the women. Razor gripped his chest and stepped back, nodding in their direction.

"Alright, fuck, I'll wait over here with Zulu and Tango. At least I know they won't bite my head off." Razor walked back toward the other men, shrugging his shoulders. Isabella laughed as the other women brought up the website, describing the items.

"I definitely want the leather bustier and chaps," she said, grinning. Taylor nodded in her direction.

"Great choice," she smiled. "I bought something similar from a shop in town, and I'm telling you, I thought Tango was going to superglue it to my body. Believe me, honey, it does the trick."

"What size are you for jeans, Bella?" asked Bree.

"Well, I've been buying size ten, but you'd have to be the judge of whether that's too tight or too loose. I can't really tell."

"I think they look perfect on you, honey. Are they comfortable?" Bella nodded. "Okay, what about tops, sweaters, that sort of thing?"

"Oh, that's more of a challenge because of my chest. I did a professional bra fitting, and I'm a 38DD, so it's tough to get things to fit sometimes. I'm usually a medium, but because of my chest, I have to get a large." Bree nodded, pecking away on the keys.

"Okay, we've got plenty in the cart for you to try when it comes. Whatever doesn't fit, we'll mail it back, sweetie."

Bella nodded, looking across the table and seeing a halo of red and one of gold. She rubbed her eyes and then looked down. Looking up again, she saw the blur more clearly.

"Bella? Are you okay, hun?" asked Gabi.

"Yea, yea, I just... sometimes, I can see shadows and filters of color. Do you guys have red and white hair?" she asked. Gabi laughed, looking at Bree.

"Yea, hun. My hair is an almost silver-white. Bree's is a gorgeous red. You can see that?"

"Yea, I mean, not all the time, but right now, it's super clear."

"Bella? When was the last time you saw an eye care professional?" Bella said nothing, simply chewing on her bottom lip. "Honey, have you seen an eye surgeon?"

"N-no. I-I saw the doctor at the free clinic when I was first diagnosed. Then I saw someone at the university clinic when I started there, and they all said there was nothing that could be done. I don't mind seeing the colors now and then or the light. It gives me a little hope. It's the headaches that really bug me."

"Headaches?" asked Gabi. "Sweetie, did you ever see a neurologist? Maybe someone else about the issues." She shook her head, the long brown tresses swishing across her back.

"No, I mean, I didn't see a need. I didn't want to be told how blind I was. Blind is blind." There was silence at the table, and Isabella squirmed a bit in her seat, waiting for someone to break that dreaded silence.

"Wh-what's wrong? Why is no one speaking?" she asked.

"Bella, would you let me look at your eyes, maybe do a few scans, some tests?" asked Gabi.

"Wh-why?" The words came out as a whisper. She could feel the blood draining from her face, the perspiration rising on her forehead. Her hands started to shake. Surely this woman would not be so cruel to give her false hope.

"I just want to confirm some things, Bella. Listen, I don't know that I'll see anything that the other doctors didn't, but the fact that twenty years after your diagnosis, you can still see color and shadow is pretty unusual. Usually, someone with any sort of macular degeneration loses their sight completely within that time. With the headaches, I just want to look at some things."

"G-Gabi," she whispered, "d-do you think…" She felt the other woman's hands cover her own, and she startled for just a moment.

"I don't know, Bella; all I know is I'd be a shitty doctor if I didn't at least look for you. Will you allow it?" she asked.

"Y-yes, but don't tell Razor why you're looking at me. Just tell him I'm having headaches, or I want to get on birth control. I don't want to give him hope. I can't do that to him."

"Understood, sweetie, just between us girls."

CHAPTER SEVENTEEN

"What the hell do you think they're talking about?" asked Zulu. Razor laughed at his friend and shook his head.

"Don't know, don't care, brother. All I know is Bella looks happy, and the girls all look like they're having fun. They're safe. That's all I give a shit about." Zulu nodded as Whiskey and Ghost walked back toward the group, big smiles plastered on their faces.

"Did you two bastards get laid?" asked Tango.

"Hell, yes," laughed Ghost. "I'm telling you guys, those fucking books have changed everything in my house. I've got a wildcat on my hands now. I thought I was fucking happy before, but I can tell you she's doing shit now beyond my imagination, and I couldn't be happier."

The guys all sat quietly, watching the women laugh over something on the computer, then chatting softly amongst themselves. Gabi was talking in a low, hushed tone to Bella, but Razor didn't want to interfere. If she needed to tell him something, she would.

"Still no signs of Baker?" asked Zulu.

"Nope. Shred and Crash both were out today asking around, trying to see if anyone has seen him. I think he's right. He's probably hiding in plain sight, just not here."

"Where do you think he is?" asked Ghost.

"Don't know, but with the early snow, he won't be outside. He'll be inside, a hotel or motel, maybe even a bed and breakfast, and we all know there are a shit ton of those around the mountains. I don't know, man. I'd love to draw him out, but I won't put Bella in that kind of danger."

"What about Shred?" asked Zulu. "Brother was willing to do it before. Maybe he'd be willing again."

"Maybe, but damn, I don't want him dead just to pull that lunatic out." Ace stood from his stool at the outer portion of the circle of men. He shoved his hands through his black hair, realizing he probably needed a haircut, then focusing on the reason he stood.

"I have an idea," said Ace. Ghost smirked at the younger man and nodded.

"You know, Ace, you're about the most brilliant bastard I know. You're trained in as many weapons as we are, and you're a black belt in every discipline of martial arts. I sure wish when you have something to say, you wouldn't look like we're gonna rip your head off, brother. You're fucking awesome, Ace. We love you, brother, and your ideas are usually the best. So, please, proceed."

Ace stared at his team leader and friend for a minute, shuffling his feet back and forth. He didn't do well with praise, and praise from Ghost was highly coveted. It took him aback for a moment, and then remembering some of what Bree taught him, he nodded at his friend in a show of thanks and stepped forward.

"I think… I think we should try to work with the warden and see if we could use Castro as bait, Hector Castro," he said, looking at a terrified Razor. "It's not unheard of, and if we get the help of Admiral Crossing, I'm betting we could get Castro released temporarily into our custody or federal custody and have him as a guest here. Maybe say his sister is ill or she's getting married." He grinned at his friend, blushing, knowing he probably said the right thing.

"Baker hates Castro. That's who he really wants. If we can take his eyes off of Bella, then the prize is within his grasp."

Ghost looked at Ace and then around the circle at the other men. Turning back to the younger man, he stood, walking closer to him. Ace was probably six-foot-one to Ghost's six-foot-four, but Ghost was layered with hard-earned muscle, whereas Ace was lean with a runner's body. Ace swallowed, not moving back from the nearness of his boss.

Ghost slowly raised his arm, settling a firm grip to the younger man's shoulder. He squeezed twice, nodding at him.

"Do not ever be afraid to let that big brain of yours speak out loud, brother. I trust you with the lives of everyone in this building. It's a brilliant suggestion. Follow through with Admiral Crossing." Ace nodded, a small grin slipping from his lips as Ghost lowered his hand. He took two steps back, and Ace nodded again, still grinning as he walked toward his office.

"Hell. Fucking, Yea," smiled Razor.

CHAPTER EIGHTEEN

"You want me to what?!" yelled the voice of Admiral Crossing.

"I need you to help secure the release of Hector Castro from Eastern Pennsylvania Correctional Facility. Temporarily. We'll guarantee his return, or you can send a federal guard with him. If we have him here, Gavin Baker will come, and we will get Gavin Baker."

Ace waited for a response, hearing the heavy breathing of the Admiral on the other end of the line. He wondered if perhaps the older man was having health issues the way he was fighting for enough air in his lungs.

"Jesus, you boys sure don't mind asking for the moon, do you?"

"You said you were willing to help us, sir, if we helped you. We need for Gavin Baker to be caught and neutralize the threat against Isabella Castro."

"Wait, Isabella Castro? How is she related?"

"Hector's sister." He heard the huff on the other end of the line and then a chuckle that turned into a full-blown belly laugh.

"Okay, who's in love with the girl?" he asked.

"Razor."

"No shit." He could almost hear the wheels turning on the other end of the line. "Do you really believe this guy will show up for Hector?"

"He blames him for his castration." There was silence on the other end, then a decisive squeak as Crossing sat in his big desk chair.

"Explain, Ace."

Ace spent the next ten minutes explaining the relationship between Baker, Black, and how Castro played into all of that. He also told him of the other inmate, Tank, who was now dead, or they would have gladly used him instead.

"Listen, son. I know Ghost. He's not going to allow this man to come to your compound and endanger everyone living there. Where do you propose doing this? And you do know that the girl, Isabella, she's going to have to be near for Baker to buy into this."

"Yes, sir. We know. We're prepared to create a plan for all of this. We own a home, a property that previously belonged to Whiskey's wife's uncle. We use it as a retreat or weekend getaway. It's in the middle of nothing except marshland on the Chesapeake, and at this time of year, it would be nothing but snow."

"Alright, Ace. Let me see what can be done. What exactly were the charges against Castro?"

"Uh, well, he had six counts of voluntary manslaughter." He heard the whistle and cussing on the end of the phone and winced at the language, and that was saying a lot, considering he was a sailor.

"You don't ask for much, do you? Give me a few days to see what I can do. Tell Ghost if I do this, you boys owe me one."

"I'll tell him." He ended the call, turning in his chair to face the fifteen men waiting, arms crossed. "Give him a few days, but we'll owe him one."

Ghost nodded. Of course, they'd owe him, the rotten bastard. He couldn't do this just as a favor for them. Fine. They'd play it his way. They'd owe him one, and then one day, he was going to owe them a big one.

CHAPTER NINETEEN

Gavin looked at the mess on his bed and sighed. How would he ever explain this? Perhaps, he could wrap the girl in the sheets and blanket, get her into his vehicle, and then maybe just take her somewhere like a date. He actually chuckled at himself. A date with a dead girl. That was funny.

Putting his plan in motion, he rolled the girl in the sheet first, then wrapped the blanket around her, securing it with duct tape. He waited patiently for an opportunity to carry her to his car, then tossed her inside the trunk, ensuring that he wasn't seen. He casually walked toward the motel office.

He opened the door to a blast of warm air, a small television on in the corner. Tapping the small bell on the desk, he waited for the night clerk. Dressed in a pair of blue jeans and blue sweatshirt, a young woman appeared. Her wire-rimmed glasses looked old-fashioned on her face. Her nail polish was chipped, but she had clear skin and nice curves. Already feeling his body hum, he smiled at the girl.

"Hi, is the manager here," he asked.

"Oh, no, sir. The manager is my dad. He and my mom went to a holiday party tonight, so I'm covering. My name is Diane. Can I help you with something?" He gave his best playboy smile and leaned on the desk.

"Well, Diane, that's a beautiful name, by the way." She blushed, and he continued. "I'm embarrassed to even say this, but I was eating my takeout on the bed and spilled it everywhere. Unfortunately, red sauce and red wine do not make for a pretty picture."

"Oh, it's fine, really. You wouldn't believe some of the messes people make sometimes. It's awful really. I can get you another set of sheets and a blanket. Unfortunately, all of our housekeeping staff is gone, and I'm the only one up here, so you'll have to change the sheets for yourself, but I can be sure and give you a twenty-dollar credit for tonight if that works." She moved through the door behind her reaching up on the shelf to grab the sheets and blanket. As she raised her arms, the skin of her abdomen could be seen, and he sighed with desire, heat pooling in his belly once more.

"Now, that is very kind of you, Diane. Truly. Completely unnecessary, but again, my thanks. I don't mind making the bed. I've made more than a few beds while serving our great country in the Middle East."

"Oh, you're a veteran?" she asked, smiling. He nodded.

"Proudly served for ten years before an unfortunate injury forced me out." His dire expression made her frown, reaching across the counter and patting his hand.

"Well, thank you for your service, sir. We honor our veterans around here, and I'll make sure Dad knows. We always make it a practice to discount the room rate." He smiled at her, nodding gravely.

"You've been so very kind to me, Diane. Is there anything at all I can do for you?" he asked.

"Oh, no, sir," she said sweetly. "It's been my honor to help. My folks will be back here soon, and I'll make sure to tell Dad." Gavin nodded, looking at the clock behind her. Damn! It was after midnight, so she was probably right. Her parents would be walking back in any time now. Sweet little Diane would have to wait for another night.

"Alright then," he said, grabbing the linens, "thank you again. I'm sure I'll see you soon." She waved as he stepped outside into the cold and made his way around the back of the building to his room. He made the bed, tucking the corners in perfectly, just as the Army taught him.

An hour later, he was driving the body of his friend to her final resting place.

"Don't worry. Oh darn, call me embarrassed. I don't even remember your name," he laughed. "No matter, I'll find a lovely place for you to lie your head for the final time. I'm quite familiar with this area now, you know." He looked back toward the trunk, unable to see the body but knowing it was there.

"Yes, indeed, I've been driving these roads for weeks now, picking out the perfect spots for all my plans. You know? It's fascinating how open people are with strangers these days. I mean, they don't know me from Adam, and yet they're willing to tell me about great little romantic spots to be alone with my love. Just crazy, don't you think, Ellie. No, that's not it. It will come to me."

Stopping the car at the small lookout point, he scanned the road both ways an as predicted, saw nothing. It was after midnight in the middle of fucking nowhere. What would any self-respecting person be doing out this way? He laughed again.

"I'm cracking myself up tonight," he said. Lifting her body over his shoulder, he leaned slightly over the steel barrier and pushed the body, watching it hit trees and rocks, falling down the embankment.

"A beautiful space to rest for eternity. You have trees and mountains. There's a stream that way, and, oh, look, Frances! That's it. Frances dear, look that way, and you'll see a lovely old cemetery. You're only off by a few miles."

Whistling on the drive back, he felt lighter, happier than he had the last few days. As he finally parked his car, he stood and stretched. Above the office was the small apartment for the owner, his wife, and daughter. In the window, he could see her small frame pulling the sweatshirt over her head, then turning off the light.

"Naughty girl," he smiled. "Naughty, naughty, girl, but I got the hint, precious."

CHAPTER TWENTY

It wasn't even six a.m. when Razor received a text to meet downstairs in the kitchen immediately. Slowly sliding out of the bed so as not to wake Isabella, he pulled on his jeans and t-shirt, not even bothering with his shoes. As he moved down the steps, he noticed Skull, Ice, Axe, and Blade dressed the same, coming in right behind him. Walking into the kitchen, George looked down and rolled his eyes.

"That's just nasty!" he said. "Wear you damn shoes in my kitchen!"

"George, take it easy, man. We were all just pulled out of bed," said Razor. He gave a loud huff as Ghost walked in with Whiskey, Zulu, and Gunner, followed by Doc and Tango.

"The whole gang?" asked Skull.

"Yea," growled Ghost. "Believe me, I do not want to be up this early. JT is teething, and we're not getting any sleep at all. Hawk and Eagle just left. The body of Frances Hillman was found in a ravine twenty-one miles from here early this morning by a father and his two sons. They were out hunting for wild turkeys. She was brutally and savagely beaten, raped, and killed. Her body was wrapped in a sheet and blanket, similar to what you would see in hotels."

"Raped? But…" Ghost held up his hand.

"We know, but use your head. He could have done it with something else." The men all nodded.

"What kind of support do they need?" asked Skull.

"None right now. If they do, they'll be calling you, Ice, and Axe. Eagle felt pretty sure he could find a trail of some sort. Appears the girl has been dead for at least three days. That could mean he's already gone from the area."

"Fuck!" growled Razor.

"Any word from the Admiral yet, Ace?" asked Whiskey.

"No, nothing yet, but he did say it would take a few days. You know," he said, looking up at Ghost and grinning, remembering his statement about speaking his mind, "he thinks he's smarter than all of us, that he knows more than we do. Hawk and Eagle are hunting him on the ground, but we need to be smarter than that. We need to start hunting him through the air."

"Through the air? Brother, I appreciate your genius, but what the fuck?" asked Gunner.

"Airwaves," he grinned. "He's spending money. How? He doesn't have any. He doesn't have a job. Gavin Baker is using an assumed identity or stolen credit cards. He has to be. We have to find out what that identity is and follow the trail."

Ghost grinned at the young man again and nodded.

"Do it. Everyone, let Ace do his thing, and he will be responsible for giving everyone their assignments." Ace looked up and started to speak, but Ghost held up a hand. "Anyone have an issue with that?"

Every man shook his head, smiling at Ace.

"Good, let's try to get another hour…" Looking at the clock, he saw it was now almost seven. "Fuck, George? Can you make some coffee?"

"This ain't a diner! Damn coffee's been ready. Pour yourself a cup and sit."

CHAPTER TWENTY-ONE

The ladies were up to something, but Razor couldn't put his finger on what it might be. They'd been huddled together on and off for three days, and it had nothing to do with the upcoming holiday dinner. The problem for Razor was that he thought it was more than one thing they were scheming over just by the sheer number of women involved.

"What's with the sour look on your face?" asked Whiskey.

"Them," said Razor, nodding his head to the table of women.

"What do you mean?"

"I mean, they've been talking in secret on and off for a few days now, and it's starting to bug me. First, it was Bella and Gabi. Then it was all of them; now it's just Bella, Gabi, and Grace, but a while ago, it was Taylor, Kat, and Darby. They're planning something, and I don't like it one bit." Razor folded his arms across his chest and frowned.

"You're acting like a child," said Whiskey, grinning at his friend. "So, they have secrets and are planning something? Big deal. We sit around here talking about all of them. Planning shit that has to do with their safety, and we never include them. Believe me, I've had more than an earful from Kat many nights."

Zulu nodded at his brothers and then looked at the table of women again.

"You know, I watch them and think about how fucking lucky we are. All those missions overseas, all the bullshit we've had to do; the times we didn't think we'd make it home and sitting over there are the most remarkable women on the planet who chose our fucked-up asses." He grinned at Whiskey and Razor, shaking his head.

"I don't know what they're planning and, frankly, I don't give a fuck. I know that the combined intelligence and brainpower at that table is greater than all of us possess together. They could be plotting the takeover of the universe, and I wouldn't give a shit. I'm fucking grateful every damned day."

Whiskey nodded at his friend, thumping Razor on the back. A cold wind blew into the restaurant as the big double doors opened. A woman in a long black coat, tall black riding boots, and a knit hat walked in. She looked around, then seeing the table of women, nodded.

"Who is that?" asked Razor.

"No clue," said Zulu, shrugging his shoulders. The woman appeared to be in her late fifties, perhaps early sixties, with a few fine lines around her big hazel eyes. When she removed the hat, her auburn

hair was cut in a sassy, short style, the front longer than the back. She

wore black leggings tucked into her knee-high boots and a hip-length

ivory sweater that hugged her plump curves.

"She related to one of the girls?" asked Razor. The other men all

shrugged again. Gabi stood and disappeared to the back of the barn and,

a few minutes later, walked out with George.

"Oh, damn, I smell a set-up." The three men stood and moved

silently to take position at a closer table, listening to every word of the

conversation.

"George, this is my friend, Mary. Mary, this is George."

"It's a pleasure to meet you, ma'am," said George with a big smile

taking in the woman before him. She was beautiful, and everything about

her made George feel suddenly twenty years younger.

"The pleasure is mine, George," she smiled in return. "Gabi and

Darby have been telling me of your exceptional cooking, and I would love

to pick your brain about some recipes. I've been trying to write a

cookbook for years about men who have made professions of cooking.

Not professional chefs, mind you, true cooks who work for restaurants or cook for large groups or catering events. When the girls told me about you, I just had to meet you."

"Well, I'm mighty honored," he grinned. "Are you a chef, Miss Mary?"

"Me? No, I can barely cook to ensure I don't starve to death. I'm actually a retired teacher. It's how I met the girls. They were interviewing for a nanny, and I told them what I was working on."

"A nanny, you say?" said George, looking at the woman.

"Yes, I never had children of my own, never married," she blushed. "I've always worked as a nanny for others, so I'm hoping the ladies will decide to take me on to watch the children and help home-school Calla when special circumstances arise."

"I see," said George thoughtfully. "Well, I find it hard to fathom how such a beautiful woman could have never been married, but stranger things have occurred."

"Why, George," she smiled, "I do believe you're flirting with me."

"Yes, ma'am, I sure am. Would you like to see the kitchen? I'm working on a pot roast for tonight's dinner special, and it's almost done."

She stood, taking his outstretched hand, and the pink hue on her cheeks turned flame red.

"I would be honored to set foot in your kitchen, George. Ladies? Can we speak after about the children? I'd love to meet them and talk more about the opportunity."

"Of course," smiled Gabi. "Please, go with George and get acquainted. We're not going anywhere."

Mary took George's big hand, and he gave her a twirl as if he was leading her onto a dance floor. She let out a giggle as if she were fifteen again, and George tucked her hand in the curve of his elbow. As they disappeared toward the back of the barn, the women all stood hugging and high-fiving one another. Behind them, Whiskey, Razor, and Zulu watched with folded arms and scowls on their faces.

"What the fuck was that?" asked Zulu. Gabi jumped and turned to look at her husband.

"Oh, hello, handsome," she grinned.

"Don't handsome me, Gabrielle. What the fuck was that?"

"We were interviewing a potential nanny to help with the children. Actually, we've pretty much decided we're hiring Mary, but we thought she and George might have a lot in common. That's all." She smiled up at Zulu, and he shook his head.

"Ladies," said Razor, touching the shoulder of Bella, "you're not fooling anyone. We know exactly what you're doing. George has been alone a long time. He doesn't want or need female companionship. I know you think you're helping, but…"

Razor's words stopped when a laughing George and Mary stepped into the restaurant, her arm still safely tucked into his elbow. He pressed a kiss to her temple, and she did the same in return. George might be in his seventies, but he was still a tall, muscular man, appearing to be the epitome of virility. Mary, suspected to be sixtyish, was attractive, intelligent, and definitely filled out a sweater.

"Hi, George, Mary," said Darby with a sly grin. "Done in the kitchen already?"

"Actually," said George, "Axe is taking over in the kitchen for me. The roast is almost done, so he can do the rest. Mary and I discovered we have quite a bit in common, so we're going into town, grab some dinner out for a change. We'll be back soon.

"Zulu? Would you mind making sure the room next to mine is ready for Miss Mary? It will be far too late for her to head home this evening when we return. I want to make sure she's safe." George smiled down at the woman, and she nodded.

"You're such a gentleman, George. Thank you. Shall we go?" He nodded, leading her to the front door as the men stood with their mouths open, watching him. At the front door, he said something to her and then turned, quickly walking back to the table of men.

"Close your mouth before you catch flies, Zulu. That's how you pick up a woman. Don't wait up," he said with a wink. "Ladies?"

"Yes, George?" they said in unison.

"Thank you."

CHAPTER TWENTY-TWO

As the men filtered into the meeting room for the regular Monday morning event, a familiar face filled a chair along the walls. Ghost, Whiskey, and Razor spoke in a low register to the man, his stiff bearing reminiscent of younger days. Admiral Mike Crossing's career was the stuff of legends. Commanding not only several ships but Special Forces teams and a stint at the pentagon.

"Did anyone see what time George got home last night?" asked Zulu with a frown.

"Yea, man, brother crawled in around three a.m. Said he and Mary went dancing last night. Dancing? Where the fuck could they go dancing until three a.m.?" asked Hawk.

"I don't think he meant that kind of dancing," growled Zulu.

"Alright, everyone, take a seat," said Ghost. "For those of you who don't know this man, let me introduce you to Admiral Mike Crossing, retired."

"Just Mike," he said, smiling at the men.

"Admiral, Mike, has agreed to try and help us with this situation involving Baker and Castro." The older man nodded, and Razor acknowledged the man seated on the opposite side of the table.

"It took a lot of string-pulling, but we got the feds and the warden to agree to allow us access to Castro. It's going to take some serious coordination, and they are not giving us one inch on this. Five U.S. Marshals will be assigned to him. They know they have to appear to be Steel Patriots and have agreed to dress in the proper attire."

"Sooo, no khakis and polo shirts?" smirked Eagle.

"No, no, khakis," said Mike. "Two of you will be with them when he is released. He will be brought to the Chesapeake property in a bullet-proof van. Once he is released into your custody, safely at Chesapeake, a message will be sent to the news media stating he was allowed a special furlough to see his sister, who is gravely ill."

"I hate even saying those words," said Razor.

"I know," said Mike, nodding, "but it's the only way. We want Baker to think that she's not able to get out and about. First, it stops him from trying to chase her down, and if she's already ill, it takes the adventure and fun out of it for him. I know that's sick, but that's how he operates. Two, it makes him think that Castro will be easy pickings.

"Now, here's what you all need to know before you agree to this. If Castro escapes, you will be held responsible and will face charges. If Castro dies under mysterious circumstances and you cannot produce a body, you will still face charges. If Castro harms or kills anyone while out, you will be held responsible."

"So basically, we're fucked if he does anything," said Hawk.

"Yes."

"Lovely, always good to know where we stand," said Ghost, grimacing. "I hate this fucking shit. Hate it. Baker should be easier to catch. My two best trackers followed him around those mountains and nearly had him twice. He's getting by us by the skin of his teeth, and I need to figure out how."

"He's getting help," said the voice from the doorway. All eyes turned toward Ace and waited for him to finish. "Someone is helping this guy. He's used three different stolen credit cards, obviously stolen cash along the way, vehicles, but someone is helping him get from one location to another. Who?" Razor shook his head, looking at Ace.

"No clue, man. I mean, Black is dead. His father is dead. His brother hates him."

"You're focusing on men," said Ace. Murmurs around the table drowned out Ace's attempts to speak until Ghost rapped the table with his knuckles, giving a nod to Ace to continue. "We know that the last girl he attacked withdrew her claim of rape but was then hit by a vehicle, most likely Baker. The cousin is still catatonic and unable to speak. We all know that sexual offenders like Baker have more than a few victims and are master manipulators. He's most likely attacked dozens of women, if not more, in his lifetime. We're missing someone. Someone whom he wrote to while serving his time, either a former victim or someone else. He convinced that poor young woman to retract her claim of rape, so we know that he has a manipulative power that we're unaware of."

"So, what are you suggesting?" asked Razor. "I mean, if these other women didn't make claims of rape, how are we supposed to know who it might be?"

"The prison has to keep track of all incoming and outgoing mail." Ace pulled out a folder with stacks of printed materials. "Everything in here is a record of letters that were sent out by Baker, and the few that were returned. He wrote to more than a dozen women."

"All women he attacked?" asked Zulu.

"No, some were just women he met online."

"Are you fucking with me?" asked Razor. "Are you telling me there is an online dating site where you can date people in prison? How the fuck does that even work?"

"Easy. The women and men find lonely prisoners through several different websites and start out as pen pals. Eventually, the communication either ceases or it increases to include visits and sometimes even conjugal visits. Baker never had a conjugal visit for obvious reasons. However, he had five women who were interested in something long-term with him."

"I can't even wrap my head around this shit," said Whiskey.

"There's actually a reality show about what happens when they are released and how the relationships progress. Most are scammers, looking for someone to support them until they can find their way to something else. The pen pals, the ones on the other end of this, tend to be lonely individuals who can't find love any other way. All of these women are over the age of forty. Keep in mind, Baker is just twenty-nine. Not that it's wrong, just that it's unusual."

"Where are these women, Ace?" asked Ghost.

"Two are in Virginia, one in West Virginia, one in North Carolina, and one in Pennsylvania. They are far enough apart that they wouldn't become aware of one another if he were doing drop-ins or visits. Also, he could easily use them as home base, flipping to a different one each night."

"What if we put something out on the news that he was in violation of his parole? Maybe say that he was wanted for questioning?" asked Mike. Ghost and the others all shook their heads.

"No, no way," said Razor. "We put anything on the wires that he's wanted, and he'll go underground. We have to figure out how these women are helping him and then get it to stop."

"How do we do that without putting the women in danger?" asked Ice. "I mean, if they're providing his meal ticket, and it stops, he could get violent with them."

"Send them all on a vacation," said Ace. "Talk to these women. My guess is they're not stupid. They're lonely and afraid. Once you speak with them, letting them know just how dangerous he is, offer them a week in Miami or something. We can afford to fly them down there and put them up for the week."

"Fucking awesome work, Ace," said Ghost. "Alright, let's take a look at the communications between the women and Baker. Once we have that done, let's split into teams and visit these ladies."

CHAPTER TWENTY-THREE

Isabella sat perfectly still as Gabi shone the light into her eyes, trying to get a clearer view at the anomaly she'd seen just a few days before. Without being able to perform a scan in the office, she was having to rely on her own instruments, which just weren't good enough.

"Well?" asked Bella.

"I'm not seeing what I saw a few days ago, and I don't understand why," she said with frustration. "We need scans and things I don't have at my fingertips, and unfortunately, right now, those men aren't going to let you out of their sight. I think we have to be patient here, Bella. Once they get Baker, and they will get him, we'll be free to head to Baltimore."

"What's in Baltimore?" asked Bella.

"A colleague whom I graduated medical school with. She went into ophthalmic surgery, and she's the best in the country. I've called her to tell her what I've seen so far and what your diagnosis and history are. She feels confident that she can give you back at least some of your vision."

"I-I can't get my hopes up," said Bella, shaking her head, "I just can't. When Hector walked me into that free clinic, I'll never forget how cold that doctor was. He just looked at us and said, 'she'll be blind for life. Get her a dog.' Who says those kinds of things to a child?"

"Obviously an asshole," said Gabi, grimacing. "Listen, honey, I can't guarantee anything, neither can my friend, but what I do know is that something is going on that I believe has been missed. The question becomes whether or not we can do anything about it."

Bella nodded, standing from the table, and reaching for Taco, never more than a few inches from her. Bundling up in their coats, the women headed out the back of the clinic onto the property and then along the walkway leading to the restaurant.

"Oh my," said Gabi with a big smile.

"What?" asked Bella.

"I see our friend, Mary, heading into the restaurant again. That's every night this week they've seen each other, and she lives almost thirty miles away."

"Wow, we really did it, didn't we?" said Bella, following the woman into the barn. "Are they out here?"

"Yes, he's giving her a big hug. Oh, oh my, he's giving her a big kiss, a big, big kiss," said Gabi, whispering to the other woman.

"This is so exciting," whispered Bella. "It's like we're creating our own CC Robat romance."

"I know. Oh, wow, he just grabbed her ass," Gabi snickered. "Oh hell, she just ground her hips into his."

"Damn, I wish I could see this," said Bella.

"You don't need to with the play-by-play." Bella and Gabi jumped a mile at the deep voice of Ghost in their ears. "Ladies."

"Shit, Ghost. Did you have to sneak up on us like that?" said Gabi.

"No, I didn't. Ladies, I appreciate what you all schemed to do with George. Lord knows, the man deserves some happiness in his life. But you've done what you wanted to do. You introduced them; you've helped it along. Now, let it go. Let it develop or not."

"You're right," said Bella. "I'm sorry, Ghost, but it was just so much fun to try and help them. I mean, Mary is amazing, and George deserves to have a woman in his life that appreciates all the things he does."

"I hear you. Really, I do."

"They're coming this way," whispered Gabi to Bella, who stood straighter, smiling at her friend.

"Hi, George, Mary, it's nice seeing you again," said Ghost.

"Ghost, ladies, I'd like to ask if I can have the suite next to mine permanently. Mary has agreed to becoming the nanny for the children, and we'd like to make sure our situation is permanent as well."

"You're getting married?" asked Ghost with shock and surprise.

"No," said Mary. "We both agree we don't need to be married to solidify our relationship. George is seventy-seven. I'm sixty-five. It's not like we're planning on a family other than all of you." She grinned at the women and winked.

"Right, yes, of course," stuttered Ghost. "So, you'd be living together?"

"Is that a problem?" asked George, looking at Ghost with a bit of disappointment and anger. Ghost held up both hands, shaking his head.

"No, no, not at all. I'm sorry if I gave you that impression. The answer is yes, of course, you can have the suite next to yours permanently. Let's get Grant up here and see if we can get that wall torn down and create the space you two really want. You know, George, you could always build on the property as well."

"I know, and I thank you for that. Mary and I spoke about it, but we don't want all the upkeep of a house. I don't want to do a yard, and she doesn't want to have to clean two thousand square feet of dust bunnies. With the two suites combined, it should be roughly around eight hundred square feet. Plenty for the two of us."

"You got it, George, and congratulations," said Ghost, gripping his hand.

"Truth is, we owe all this to the girls for getting us together," said Mary. "I mean, I was just looking for more information on my cookbook when I ran into Darby at the bookstore and got talking about my history as a nanny. It just seemed perfect."

"Yea, perfect," smirked Ghost. "Well, we're happy you're here, Mary, and I sure hope you and George will be happy together."

"Thank you, Ghost." Mary and George walked to a small table in the corner where Axe set their dinner down, grinning at them.

"Alright, ladies," said Ghost, shaking his head in resignation with a big grin on his face, "well done. Well done."

CHAPTER TWENTY-FOUR

"Hi, Amanda," said Ice, walking toward the bar. The beautiful college girl was home for the holiday break, and Ice could not have been happier. They'd shared nothing more than a few chaste kisses and hugs, but he knew that this girl was his.

He'd forced himself to take it slow with her, knowing that not only was she naïve and young, she was also a virgin. He wanted her to have choices in her life, and if they started a relationship, her choice would be him either by default or out of a belief that she owed him something. Blessed with the voice of an angel, she deserved the opportunity to pursue a professional singing career if she so desired or to play her violin for thousands in a symphony hall.

"Hi, Decker, I mean, Ice," she smiled.

"I've told you that you can always call me Decker. Are you glad to be home for break?" he asked. Amanda nodded, gracing him with a big smile.

"I am. I'll only have about three weeks left after Thanksgiving, and I will officially have my degree in music. I have no clue what I'm going to do with it, but I'll have it," she laughed.

"Well, I'm sure you'll figure all that out. You got everything you need for the bar?" She nodded at him and smiled again, hoping he would take the flirtation as a sign that she would really like to be kissed. "Good, that's good. Okay, so, ummm, let me know if you need anything."

Ice turned and walked toward the table with Hawk, Eagle, Razor, and Whiskey. Plopping in the vacant seat, he blew out a breath. Looking up at the faces around the table, he threw his hands in the air.

"What? What the hell are you all looking at?" he growled.

"Brother," said Razor, "dying of blue balls is painful."

"What the fuck? That's Amanda, remember? Innocent, sweet, virgin Amanda."

"Yea, we get that, really we do," said Whiskey. "But, brother, every woman loses her virginity sooner or later. Now, the ideal situation is the woman chooses who it is she gets to lose that virginity with. From the looks she was giving you, I'd say she's made her selection."

"What the hell are you talking about?" he growled.

"Christ, you're thick as fuck," said Hawk. "She walked in here two hours ago and asked where you were. I told her you would be returning shortly. An hour later, she asked me again. I said shortly. Fifteen minutes ago, she saw you walk in the door. She immediately fluffed her hair, put on some lip gloss, and plastered on a smile that would light a fucking city. Now, I've said this before if you don't want that girl, then she's fair game for me."

Ice slid his chair back and gripped the throat of Hawk, squeezing ever so slightly. Eagle stood but didn't make a move, mostly because his idiotic twin brother had a grin on his face even as he was losing the ability to breathe.

"I've told you to stay away from her," he growled.

"Then you need to fucking claim her," rasped Hawk. All eyes suddenly were on something or someone behind Ice as he let go of Hawk's throat.

"Hi, Amanda," said Razor. "How are you, honey?"

"Hi, Razor, I'm good. I like Isabella, by the way. We only met for a few minutes, but she's really sweet."

"Thank you, honey," he grinned, looking from her to Ice.

"Uh, Decker, I mean, Ice, can I speak to you for a minute?" Ice nodded. "Eagle? Will you watch the bar?"

"Sure, hun," he said, rising from the table.

Ice followed Amanda as she moved toward the back of the barn, walking up the stairs to the private quarters. She opened the door to her room and waved him inside.

"Is everything okay? Is something wrong with your room?" he asked. Amanda turned, her arms folded beneath those perfect breasts.

"Am I ugly, Decker?"

"Wh-what?" You could have hit him with a shovel, and he would have been less shocked than he was by her question.

"I asked you if you thought I was ugly."

"No, why in the hell…"

"Do you not like my body?" she asked.

"Amanda…"

"Do I smell? Is my hair the wrong color?"

"Amanda, stop!" he yelled, gripping her upper arms. "What the fuck are you going on about? You know I think you're beautiful, honey. I love your body, and I love your hair and your eyes…"

"Then what the fuck is wrong?" He looked at her confused, searching her face for some sort of clue. "I've given you every signal, every sign to say I want you. I'm ready, and you've done nothing."

"You... you want me?"

"Oh my God! Yes, Decker! I've wanted you from the moment I saw you months ago! I've waited patiently for you to do something other than just kiss me like I'm your damn sister. I want you, Decker, but if you don't want me, please tell me now so I stop acting like such a lovesick puppy!"

She really wanted him. Holy shit, this beautiful, talented, amazing creature actually wanted him. Decker stepped closer, his arms sliding from her upper arms to her shoulders, one hand gripping the back of her neck, the other falling to her hip.

"I'm a fucking fool," he said, taking another step. "I wanted to give you time to change your mind, honey. To find some nice college boy that you have more in common with than some ex-sailor/biker."

"Decker, everything I want is right here," she said, moving closer, her body now pressed against his. "All I want is to work in this bar, sing once in a while, and be in your arms every night. That's all, Decker."

"What about your music lessons?"

"Darby is going to let me teach lessons in the space above the bookstore. I can convert the two bedrooms into sound studios and even allow kids to record their own music. I get it all, Decker. I get to be here with you, play my music, and teach. I don't need some college guy who's more interested in carving notches on his bedpost than carving my initials in a tree." He smiled at that, kissing her forehead.

"Decker McManus, if you kiss me like that one more time, I'm going to go downstairs and ask Hawk to take me on a date and..." Slam. His lips crashed against hers, their tongues dancing as he ground his hips into her own. She felt the long stiff rod against her belly and moaned, letting her fingers glide through his hair.

Amanda slowly raised her leg, letting it glide up his, her warmth searing his jeans. Decker gripped her ass and pulled her tighter against him.

"Fuck, Amanda, baby, we have to stop, or I won't be able to. I want to, but I want to take our time, not be in a rush." She nodded, smiling.

"So, you want me?" she asked, blushing.

"Fuck baby, I want all of you all the time, Amanda, all the time. Tonight, we'll talk more here or in my room, doesn't matter. You're mine, Amanda." She tilted her head back and let out a loud laugh.

"Finally!" she smiled, kissing him again. Decker grinned at her, and then his gaze wandered to the nightstand to see the newest book in the series by CC Robat.

CHAPTER TWENTY-FIVE

Skull and Axe knocked on the door of the small ranch-style home of Janet Birnbaum. Janet was the first of the women it appeared Baker made contact with, although they couldn't find the connection through www.barstostars. He couldn't understand what the fucking attraction was for anyone to get to know someone behind bars, but he also wasn't going to judge.

As a former lieutenant in the Coast Guard, Skull had seen more than a few scary things in his day. Rescuing refugees from high seas, confiscating yachts full of drugs, or plucking some stupid fuck off his sailboat in a hurricane. This, however, was not something he'd trained for.

"Can I help you?" asked the woman standing behind the screen door. She was easily in her mid-forties, short and rather plump around the middle. Her graying, brown hair was cut close to her head, her brown eyes hidden behind thick glasses.

"Janet Birnbaum?" asked Skull.

"Yes, Rabbi Birnbaum," she said, smiling.

"Rabbi? Right, ma'am, my name is Scott Crawford, and this is my friend, Axel Mains. Ma'am, we'd like a moment of your time to speak to you about Gavin Baker."

She smiled at the two younger men and nodded.

"Gavin's not here right now. He left a few days ago to visit with a sick friend in West Virginia." Skull nodded as Axe texted the team headed to West Virginia.

"Yes, ma'am. Please, can we come in? This is important." She nodded, opening the door for the men. Skull noticed the cleanliness of the home and cursed under his breath. He didn't want to remove his boots, but he felt certain Rabbi Birnbaum would ask him to. He started to take them off, and she shook her head.

"No need, young man," she smiled. "Wood floors make it easy to clean everything. Let's sit in the kitchen, and I'll make you some tea." She busied herself with the tea kettle while Skull and Axe took their seats, laying their jackets on the back of the chairs.

"So, what is this about Gavin?"

"Can you tell us how you met Gavin?" asked Skull.

"Oh, yes, I was doing prison ministry work. Several clergies in the area rotate in and out of many of the prisons. Sometimes, we go in as a collective group. Other times, it's just one of us."

"I don't understand," said Axe. "He isn't Jewish."

"No, but he was willing to explore the faith. I was happy to have some private discussions with him about Judaism, and he was a very quick student. We started writing letters, and, well, one thing led to another." Both men solemnly nodded. "I know what you're thinking. Older woman, younger man, he's leading me astray, or I'm leading him astray."

"No, ma'am," said Skull. "I promise that's not what we're thinking at all."

"No? Well, you'd be the first. My children think he's out to take all my money, although, as you can see, it's not as if I'm independently wealthy. I make a modest living. I have a modest savings from my husband's life insurance, and I make extra income by doing some counseling and such."

"I see, and did you give Gavin any money?" asked Axe.

"I, well, he just got out of prison. He needed money for clothing and such, so of course, I gave him some spending money. It was the decent thing to do. Poor man, you know he can't... perform... in the bedroom the way others do. He thought that would matter to me, but a woman my age knows that there are other things far more important."

"Yes, ma'am," said Skull. "Ms. Birnbaum..."

"Janet," she smiled.

"Janet, Gavin Baker is not who he seems to be," he said carefully. He watched her face fall and the slight quiver of her lip. "Ma'am, he's a sociopathic liar, rapist, and murderer. He is responsible for the rape and mutilation of at least three women and the violent rape of his own cousin, a child at the time."

"No," she said in a heavy breath, "no, he said... he said that was all a mistake, and he was cleared of those charges."

"Janet, I do not want to have to say any of this to you, but I believe that you are in danger simply by being near Gavin Baker. I think he will come back for more money, and when it runs out, or your usefulness runs out, he will physically harm you."

The woman swallowed hard, standing to set her unused spoon in the sink. Her shoulders slumped, and she let out a long breath. Turning, she faced the two men with tears in her eyes.

"I've been a fool, haven't I?"

"Janet, you have not been a fool. Gavin Baker is a manipulator. There were four other women he made contact with while in prison, and he is using all of them at this very moment. We believe the reason he went to West Virginia was to see another woman whom he met in an online dating site."

"Oh, dear God," she whispered.

"This man, Janet, this man is trying to harm the fiancée of my brother. That young woman is blind. We only want to stop him and get him back behind bars. But we also do not want to put you in any danger." She nodded.

"What do you need from me?"

CHAPTER TWENTY-SIX

Whiskey and Tango peered out the window of the truck, checking the numbers on the rural mailboxes. The houses were far apart, barely able to see your neighbor's front porch, which would play well for Baker.

This part of North Carolina was known for backwoods stills, the birthplace of car racing, while men ran their moonshine to waiting buyers. As Whiskey stopped in front of the last mailbox, he looked up to see an older man shoveling the walkway leading to the front door of a moderate-sized log cabin.

"Is this it?" asked Tango. Whiskey nodded, a deep crevice of frown lines appearing on his forehead as he looked at the other man.

"Yea, according to the address Ace gave us, this is where she lives. I sure as fuck hope she isn't married."

"Only one way to find out. Let's go." They exited the truck and started to walk up the driveway. The man turned to see the approaching strangers, his hands gripped tightly around the shovel, watching the big men move toward him.

"Afternoon, sir," said Whiskey. "I was wondering if you could help us. We're looking for Carol Jessup."

"I'm Carol Jessup," he said. You could have knocked Whiskey over with a feather. Tango started to speak, but no words came out. "You expected me to be a woman."

"I'm sorry, sir. We did. It doesn't matter, I assure you. That's not what we're here about."

"And just what are you here about?" he asked.

"Gavin Baker." The man's spine stiffened, and he stood a little straighter, the shovel still gripped tightly between his hands.

"Wh-what about Gavin?"

"Sir, we mean you no harm," said Whiskey. He could only imagine what the two of them looked like, both over six-foot-two, both over two hundred pounds, both with beards and leather jackets. "I assure you that we only wish to speak with you. We can do it out here if you like or somewhere more public."

"No, nowhere else," he said. The man looked up and down the deserted road and then nodded at the two men. "Alright, come in." He set the shovel against the giant logs on the outside of the home. Opening the door, he waved the two men through and toward a grouping of comfortable leather furniture.

"This is a beautiful place," said Tango. "Did you build this?"

"How did you know?" he smiled. "Built it with my own two hands. Took me almost ten years to finish it. The backroom there, that was the original cabin. It belonged to my grandfather. When I decided to move back here, well, it wasn't exactly my choice, but I wanted to make a place that was all mine and mine alone."

"It's really something. Amazing craftsmanship." Carol nodded at the other men.

"I appreciate that, but I doubt very seriously if you came out here to tell me I have a nice cabin. You said this was about Gavin."

"Yes, sir. May I ask, what's your relationship with Gavin?"

"We-we started as friends, just pen pals originally. It's something I've done for years, write to both men and women who are incarcerated."

"That's admirable, but may I ask why?" said Whiskey.

"Are you gay, son?"

"No, sir."

"And you?" he asked, looking at Tango.

"No, sir. We're both married to women."

"Then you have no idea what it's like to be a gay man in rural North Carolina. It's a prison all by itself. I did time once because I was gay. As a teenager, I was caught with another man at a rest stop. At that time, having a relationship with someone of the same sex was against the law. I was arrested and sent to jail for thirty days. Thirty days with grown men. I was fifteen."

"I'm sorry, sir."

"Not as sorry as I was. I left here shortly after that. Lived all over. New York for a bit, then Chicago, and then California. That seemed to be the place I was accepted the most, so I stayed out there for quite a while. Then I got word that my grandfather was sick and dying. The only man who didn't disavow me, and I came back.

"When I started writing to Gavin, at first, it was just like any other letter I wrote. I was just trying to give him something to hold onto. He wrote to me about his early release. That the woman who'd claimed he raped her recanted her statement. I was so excited to meet him but worried too. I mean, he's a young man, and, well, I'm not." He smiled, but there was pain in his smile.

"He was so kind to me. Stayed with me for a week and then said he needed to visit some family and old friends. I didn't expect to ever see him again. I gave him a few hundred dollars to help him out and thought, well, that's that."

"Except it wasn't?" asked Tango. The older man shook his bald head.

"No. He came back, kept coming back. He couldn't have sex, wasn't able, but he allowed me to use his body for my own desires." Carol looked into the eyes of the two young men in front of him, waiting to see the hate and disgust. Instead, he saw compassion and understanding.

"I know he doesn't love me, but it's something in a place where I have nothing."

"When was the last time you saw him?" asked Whiskey.

"Three, no, four days ago. It was a fast trip. He said his brother was dying, and he had to get back to him. He needed money for gas and hotels, so I gave him another five hundred dollars." Tango nodded.

"Sir, his brother is alive and well. Perfectly healthy. Mr. Jessup, I'm sorry to have to tell you this, but Gavin Baker is not who he seems." Carol Jessup nodded, looking down at his old, wrinkled hands.

"I suspected he was too good to be true," he smiled.

"Mr. Jessup, Gavin has fooled multiple people into believing he wants a romantic relationship with them. Unfortunately, his real goal is to physically harm a young blind woman to get revenge on her brother, a man in prison. Gavin has taken money from at least four other individuals and during his freedom, murdered at least three women."

"What should I do?" asked Carol with tears in his eyes.

"We have a proposal for you."

CHAPTER TWENTY-SEVEN

Donna Viceroy watched as the two men walked toward her townhome. They were definitely a couple of cuties, and she could see herself having some fun with the two of them. One was a dark Latino, and the other was all masculine, bearded sin.

She'd been outside, hanging her Christmas lights up early this year. She'd felt in the holiday spirit, a little lighter, a little happier this year, and just knew that decorating early was going to make her feel even better.

"Afternoon, ma'am," said Ghost.

"Hello," she said, smiling at the two men. "Two handsome strangers, call me lucky. Can I help you?"

"We hope so," said Razor. "My name is Diego Salcedo, and this is Eric Stanton. We'd like to speak to you about Gavin Baker."

"Is-is something wrong? Is Gavin hurt?" she asked.

"No, ma'am, he's not hurt, but we do need to have a conversation with you about his whereabouts."

"Are you law enforcement?" They both eyed the woman suspiciously. Donna was probably in her early fifties; her hair dyed an unnatural blonde. She appeared to have an over-filled silicone chest and perhaps a few too many needles to her frozen face.

"We are not, ma'am."

"Then why are you asking about Gavin? He said he has enemies, and I should be careful who I speak with," she said, sticking out that big chest.

"Ma'am, I can assure you we are not here to hurt you in any way. We do, however, need to try and find Gavin before he hurts a young blind woman."

"I see." She nervously nibbled on her bottom lip, staring at the two men. She didn't want to believe them, but something inside her said she should.

"Ms. Viceroy, Gavin has been seeing several other individuals over the last few weeks. He's using you and these other people to get money in order to move around and stay away from the police, who are indeed trying to find him." Razor let that sink in and watched as Donna let out a long slow breath.

"He is in violation of his parole, and we suspect that he's harmed several young women," said Ghost. "Has he asked you for money?"

"He didn't ask. I offered," she said, swallowing. "He needed a car at first, and so I lent him mine. A week later, he said it was stolen. He rented a car and came back here. I got my insurance filed and got another car. The next time, he didn't ask for the use of my car. It was cash he needed to see a friend of his who is dying." Razor nodded.

"I gave him three thousand dollars." Ghost rubbed his big hand over his face and grimaced.

"I'm so sorry, ma'am," said Razor. She sat down on her front step, staring up at the two men in front of her.

"I'm an old fool. A fifty-five-year-old, thrice divorced, old fool. I was so desperate, so lonely," she hiccupped, fighting back tears. "He wrote the sweetest letters, and when I told him about our age difference, he didn't seem to care. First... first, I figured it was just a desperate inmate wanting sex, but when he told me he wasn't... isn't able, well, I just knew that it wasn't about that."

"No, ma'am, it's not about sex." Razor tried to be compassionate with the woman, but she was also helping the man who was trying to kill his own woman.

"What has he done?"

"We believe he's murdered several young women in his quest to harm a young blind woman, my fiancée," said Diego. She nodded at him apologetically. "He has crisscrossed over Virginia and West Virginia, the Carolinas, and even Pennsylvania and continues to evade police and our team, who are some of the best trackers on the planet." She nodded again, looking up at the clouded sky.

"It's going to snow again tonight." They both looked up and nodded as well. "He stays in motels, not hotels. You know, the small roadside places most people would never stay in. Never spends more than forty or fifty bucks a night on a room. I know because I let him use my credit card the first time. His hair is thinning, so occasionally, he'll wear a wig or toupee."

That was new information for both Ghost and Razor. No one mentioned that they'd seen him with more hair or that it might be a different color, but it made sense and might be one of the reasons they were unable to find him. If he was disguising his hair, he could be using other things to change his appearance.

"Ma'am, we think it might be safer if you weren't here the next time he came calling. We'd like to send you down to Miami for a week, all expenses paid by our company." She shook her head, standing, and wiped the dirt and leaves from her jeans.

"No, that's not necessary. My sister lives in the Upper Peninsula of Michigan. She wanted me to come for the holidays, so I guess this just makes up my mind for me. I'll pack up and head that way tonight." Ghost nodded at her.

"I'm really sorry, ma'am," said Razor. "I wish there was something we could say to make this easier for you. Just know that you aren't the only one who fell for Gavin's charm. I would also tell you to be very grateful we found you and stopped this before it could go any further. Again, I'm truly sorry, Ms. Viceroy."

"You know what, handsome? I do believe you are."

CHAPTER TWENTY-EIGHT

"Why did we get this gig again?" asked Hawk. His twin shook his head at him. Eagle loved his brother, but sometimes his mouth really went into overdrive. It was as if he received the gift of stealth, and his brother got the gift of gab, although most people would simply say it was the gift of being an annoying little shit.

"We're doing it for our brother, be nice."

"Whatever, what's the fucking address again?" Eagle handed him the sheet of paper as they walked along the sidewalk, small off-brand boutiques and coffee shops lining the streets. This was definitely not the nice part of town, and if anyone was living above one of the shops, they had to be fighting rat and roach problems at the very least.

"Is this it?" asked Eagle. They both looked up with raised eyebrows and frowned. "This can't be fucking it. Please tell me this is some sort of joke. I'm going to fucking kill Ace." His brother shook his head as he looked at the flashing neon sign for the Pink Slipper Senior Gentleman's Club.

They opened the outer door, and a big beefy bouncer asked for twenty bucks from each of them. Hawk looked back at his brother and grinned. Eagle pulling out the forty dollars, handed it to the man.

Opening the main door, they both squinted, trying to adjust to the light of the room. Smoke blurred their vision, but it was also the smell of cheap whiskey, even cheaper cologne and perfume, sweat, and sex that made them take a step back.

"We both know I'm a man-whore. I like pussy better than even you, and you're my twin, but I am not touching seventy-year-old snatch," he said, staring at the wrinkled old woman grinding her sagging, tasseled breasts against the man at the edge of the stage.

"Shit, these old fucks are gonna have a heart attack," said Eagle.

"Don't look now, but they're not all old. I see at least a dozen guys our age and maybe another dozen in their thirties and forties. What am I missing? Is this some new trend that we missed?" Granny finished her number on stage, and the announcer told everyone to hold onto their dicks as they welcome Millie Spitz.

Hawk and Eagle looked at one another and then back to the stage as a large, African American woman took the floor, shaking her rather plump ass and exceptionally large thighs at the audience.

"You don't think Millie Spitz is Mildred Spatz?" asked Eagle.

"Fuck!" growled Hawk. "Come on, let's sit down and wait until she's done." They took the last two seats two rows back from the stage and waved the waitress over, a cute little thing who couldn't be more than twenty. She had long legs, a phenomenal rack, and hot pink hair. The little black dress she wore barely covered her ass, and for just a moment, Hawk thought this might all work out.

"What can I get 'ya, sugar?" she asked.

"Your number," smiled Hawk, winking at his brother.

"Cute, what can I get 'ya?" He looked at his brother, who shrugged, and he looked back toward the girl.

"Seriously? We're the youngest guys in the room, twins, fucking rocking bodies, and you're not going to even look at me?" he said, feeling seriously deflated. She looked up, perusing their bodies, and then just shrugged.

"I'm gay. What do you want to drink?" she asked again.

"Two beers and a private dance with Millie Spitz," said Eagle. She looked at them and then back toward Millie, shrugging her shoulders again. Ten minutes later, the warm beer was gone, and Millie was standing in front of them, staring from one identical face to the other.

"You boys want a dance?" she asked incredulously.

"Yea," smiled Hawk. "Why wouldn't we?"

"Baby, I'm tired; my feet are killin' me, and I don't have time for your white-boy shit. What do you want?" She sat in the chair next to them, obviously with no intent on giving them a lap dance. Hawk's pride was taking a serious hit in this place. A place that, by all accounts, should have him as king of the hill.

"We want to talk to you about Gavin," said Eagle. She looked at both men and nodded, standing. She waved them toward a door in the back. Inside was a long purple velvet sofa that had certainly seen better days and probably had not seen a good steam cleaning since the Reagan administration.

"Have a seat," she said, taking the chair by the door. "What do you want with Gavin?"

"First of all, my name is Tyran O'Neal, and this is obviously my twin brother, Ryan."

"Ain't nothin' obvious about it, baby. All you young white boys look the same to me. Too much working out, over-inflated muscles, insane egos, and not a dick worth sucking between 'ya." Eagle raised his eyebrows and looked at his twin, who promptly stood, unzipped his fly, and pulled out the nine-and-a-half inches – soft – to prove Millie wrong.

"Well, color me impressed, white boy," she grinned. Then frowning, she immediately said, "Now, what do you want with Gavin."

"We need to find him. He's trying to hurt a young blind woman."

"Boy, can't hurt no one. He ain't got no dick," she snickered.

"Mildred…"

"Millie."

"Millie, we know that, but we're not talking about sex. Gavin has murdered several young women since his release from prison. He's been connecting with other women like yourself and getting money so he can find this blind woman. We need to stop him, but we also want to be sure you're safe." That was probably the most Eagle had spoken in the last five years. Usually, his overly talkative and obnoxious twin was the one with all the words.

"I see, and you think he's gonna hurt me," she said, eyeing the two young men.

"We think that he may try to. We'd like to ask you to go to Miami, a week paid vacation on us. It will just get you away from him and hopefully out of harm's way until we can find him."

"Well, shit." She stood and stretched her back, her huge bosoms nearly popping out of her costume. "I figured there was somethin' up. I was writin' to him just to be nice at first, and then he decides we should be more than friends. Spill his guts to me. Tells me about the misunderstanding with his cousin and the other girl, how she dropped the charges against him, and everything was fine."

"I was so flattered he'd want anything to do with me. I just fell right in with it all. Showed up here 'bout two weeks ago. Stayed with me a coupla days and then said he had to visit a sick friend. Asked me for gas money, so I gave him a few hundred dollars. All I had in cash tips. Didn't figure I'd see him again. He called yesterday and said he would be passing this way again, but it might be a few days."

"If it's any consolation to you, Millie," said Hawk, smiling at her, "I'd come back to visit with you any time."

"Well, you got a dick worth suckin', white boy, so you can come any time you like," she grinned with a tear in her eye. She bit her lip and turned away from them. "Damn! I'm an old fool."

"No, ma'am, you are not," said Eagle. "You're a compassionate woman, and maybe one day, I'll be lucky enough to find someone just like you." She nodded, smiling at him.

"Your dick look like his?" she asked. Hawk laughed, but Eagle grinned at her.

"Much better."

CHAPTER TWENTY-NINE

Gunner and Zulu wound their way through the small picturesque community outside of Gettysburg, Pennsylvania. The trees were bare, their leaves long since blown away by the harsh November winds. Small patches of snow lined the streets, but for the most part, everything was clear.

"So far, everyone seems able to convince their folks to head to Florida," said Zulu. "Sure hope we're not the ones to break the streak."

"Yea, me too, brother." He looked at the addresses and knew they were getting close. As he spotted the number they were given, his stomach sank. "Fuck. Tell me that is not the address."

"Shit. Are you fucking kidding me?" said Zulu. "A nursing home? Maybe it's someone who works there. Could we get that lucky?" Gunner parked the truck, and they hopped out, walking toward the big double glass doors. A reception desk with a group of small pumpkins on it greeted them.

"Good afternoon," said the cheery woman.

"Afternoon, ma'am," said Zulu. "My name is Quincy Slater, and this my friend and coworker, Gunner Michaels. We're looking for Alice Parker."

"Are you friends of Alice?" she asked, eyeing the two men up and down.

"No, ma'am, we don't know Miss Alice at all, but we know of someone that we believe she has befriended." The other woman nodded again, pursing her lips.

"You boys planning on stealing from that poor old woman as well," she said quietly. Zulu closed his eyes, counting to ten.

"We are definitely not," said Gunner.

Standing, the woman led them down a long hallway into one of the rooms. The small room had a full-sized bed, side table, and one comfortable recliner. There was a decent-sized television mounted on the wall, along with a few family photos.

"Miss Alice? How are you this afternoon?" asked the woman.

"Oh, hello, Joannie. I'm good, honey. Who are these handsome boys?" The woman started to speak, but Zulu stepped forward.

"Ma'am, my name is Quincy Slater, and this is my friend Gunner Michaels. We're here to ask you some questions about Gavin."

The woman took in a sharp breath, clasping her hand at her throat. Her tired blue eyes filled with tears, and Quincy kneeled his big body in front of her. Not wanting to frighten her, he took her hand gently between his two big bear paws.

"I mean you no harm, ma'am, and I certainly don't mean to cause you any duress. I was just hoping that you could maybe tell me a bit about how you came to know him."

"He's not a nice boy," she said with trembling lips.

"Yes, ma'am, we are well aware of that, which is why we're here," said Gunner. She nodded at the two men and then Joannie, silently asking her to leave them.

"I thought I would just meet a nice friend on that website. It gets so lonely here. Everyone is old like me, but every day, we're one less." Zulu still held her hand in his big ones, smiling up at her. "Gavin said his own mother rejected him, his father tossed him aside. I felt so bad for him. What parent does that!?"

"Don't know, ma'am," said Zulu. "I have twin boys, the most beautiful wife in the world. I can't imagine leaving them. Gunner over there, he's got himself a wife and little girl, prettiest family you'd ever see, so we're not the kind of men to dessert out families."

"No, no, I don't expect you are. My Alfred, he died almost ten years ago. No one tells you how lonely you'll get, how sometimes you'll turn the television and radio on just to have a whole bunch of noise around you." She shook her head and then steeled herself once more. "Gavin said he just wanted to be my friend, spend some time, and get to know me. He said he needed someone to just care about him, and, well, I needed to feel needed, I suppose."

"I don't think he knew I was in the home. He called about three weeks ago and asked to come and see me. I gave him the address and waited for him to arrive. It was after midnight when he finally got here."

"What happened?" asked Gunner.

"He was angry. Angry that I didn't tell him my living situation. He said he needed a place to stay, and obviously, I couldn't provide that for him. Asked me for money. I told him I could write him a check, and he got angry about that too, said he didn't have a valid driver's license, so he wouldn't be able to cash the check. Honestly, I was afraid for my life. One of the night nurses must have heard him. She called security, and they escorted him off-property. Since that time, I lock my door every night."

"I think that's a fine idea, ma'am," said Zulu. "Are you able to travel at all, Alice?"

"Oh no, not any longer. I need so much help, I just can't do it anymore." Zulu nodded at the woman and smiled.

"Well, ma'am, we were really hoping to send you away for a few days until we find him, but would you be agreeable to one of our teammates coming down to keep watch over you?"

"Oh my, do you really think that's necessary?" she asked.

"I'd rather not take any chances," said Gunner, smiling at the older woman. "If you were my mother or grandmother, I'd sure do everything I could to protect you, ma'am."

"Alright then, if you boys feel it's necessary. I'm grateful to have someone watch over me. Gavin really frightened me. Taught me a good lesson. I won't be using that internet again any time soon." Gunner and Zulu both chuckled at the older woman, smiling.

"Well, ma'am," said Gunner, "it is good for some things, like shopping or finding information you might need. But maybe, in the future, you stick to dating neighbors or well-known acquaintances." Alice smiled up at the handsome young man.

"You're a married man, Gunner, don't try to sweet-talk me," she grinned.

"Wouldn't dream of it, Alice, wouldn't dream of it."

CHAPTER THIRTY

"Do you think the guys will be back today?" asked Bella to the group of women. She hadn't realized how much she would miss Razor until he wasn't in her bed the first night. Having grown accustomed to his body wrapped around hers, his scent, the feel of his hard cock in the morning pressed against her backside. Yep, she'd missed him by evidence of her panties wet at just the thought of him returning.

"They're all due back any time now," said Gabi. "Ace said they were just tying up some loose ends. With Gavin's financial backers cut off from him, he won't be able to do anything other than bring himself into the light."

George stepped out from the back with a huge pot of soup, setting it in the middle of the table, Mary close on his heels. They passed around bowls to each of the women and then sliced the homemade bread. Calla was sitting on a big blanket near the table, playing with the twins and JT.

"This smells wonderful, George," said Bella.

"It's Mary's recipe," he smiled. "She taught me a thing or two about some different herbs. Amazing woman, and she's all mine."

"Oh, George," said Mary, hugging him. "You're such a flatterer. It's why I've fallen for you. That and you're a dynamo in bed!" Gabi nearly spit her soup out. Bella started coughing, and the others all sat with open mouths.

"Okay, I did not need to walk up and hear that," said Razor with Ghost. "Hi, baby, you doing okay other than the shock of knowing George is a dynamo in bed."

"I'm good," she laughed. "I missed you." She ran her fingers along his jaw, finding that beautiful mouth, she pressed her lips against him.

"So, George, you're a dynamo in the bedroom?" asked Ghost, grinning while he hugged his wife close to him, his son in his other arm.

"You young boys think you know everything. Experience is good to have and believe me, it pays off in certain areas. The bedroom happens to be one of those areas," he said, winking at Mary. She whispered in his ear, and he chuckled, turning a fine shade of pink. They walked back toward the barn, their fingers locked together. Ghost just grinned, shaking his head.

"I hope you ladies are satisfied with that little match," said Razor.

"We have no idea what you're talking about," said Grace. "Mary is our nanny, and the fact that she and George fell in love, well, I think that's just about the sweetest thing ever."

"How did the trip go?" asked Bella.

"Fine, honey, just fine. We were able to convince all five of the people to leave or be protected. Now, we need to get you to safety. We're going to head to the house in Chesapeake tomorrow. Your brother will be joining us."

"I'm anxious to visit with him again, but correct me if I'm wrong. Won't this lead Gavin right to us, to me? I mean, what's going to happen if he attacks that house and I'm inside?"

"We'll be there, baby," said Razor, kissing her forehead.

"I understand that, but I'm going to be in a new space that I'm unfamiliar with. If he attacks the house, and I have to find my way to a safe room or something, I'm going to struggle, not knowing where anything is located. Even now, having been here for several weeks, I still bump into things on occasion. Taco is good, but he can't read my mind," she said.

"Damn," muttered Ghost. "Maybe we take her down there sooner rather than later."

The doors of the restaurant opened. Hawk, Eagle, Gunner, and Zulu stepped through. Gabi took off toward her husband, leaping into his big arms, her little belly pressed against his own ripped muscles. Gripping the back of his head, she kissed him, moaning as she did.

"Damn!" he said, pulling back. "Maybe I should leave for a few days every month to get a greeting like that when I return."

"Don't you dare!" she said, kissing his face. "I missed you, and I'm so damn horny right now I can barely stand it. Get me back to the house, now."

"Fuck, I'll see y'all for dinner, maybe. I'll let Mary know we're leaving the twins here for a bit." Zulu carried her all the way through the double steel doors and off toward their home. The others all grinning. Calla was immediately in her daddy's arms, kissing his cheek.

"How's my girl? Have you been good for Mommy?" he asked.

"I've been so good, Daddy, and I've been playing with JT, Wade, and Ty. I'm helping with the babies so when you and Mommy have a baby, I'll be ready." Gunner's eyes went wide, and he looked at Darby.

"No, no, no," she said, shaking her head. "I'm not pregnant yet." Gunner had a look of both relief and disappointment, and that only made Darby smile. Razor stood Bella from her chair, then sat down, pulling her onto his lap.

"That was my seat, you know," she said, grinning.

"I know," he growled, rubbing her ass cheeks through the thin material of her leggings, "but this seat is mine, and I needed to feel it against me." Bella wound her arms around his neck, kissing him below his ear, tracing her tongue along his jaw. She felt the rumble of his chest and smiled.

"You keep doing that, baby, and I won't be able to get up."

"Funny," she said, "I think you're up right now."

"Fuck it," he said, standing and pulling her with him, "let's go upstairs and get packed for Chesapeake. We should get there early any way to get you and Taco acclimated."

As they entered their suite of rooms, Razor turned her in his arms, one hand gripping the curve of her waist, the other the swell of her breasts. His tongue found hers, dancing and swirling with desire and need, tasting the soup and homemade bread.

"I'm so wet for you, Diego," she said breathlessly, "please, I need you inside me now."

"Fuck," he moaned, pulling her sweater over her head. He unhooked the bra and took one nipple between his teeth, pulling, sucking, tasting the delicious scent of her skin. Lying her back on the bed, he pulled her boots off and then, pulling her leggings down, saw the pink satin thong.

"Fucking hell, baby, that's sexy. When did you get that?" he asked. She smiled.

"The girls helped me do some online shopping. Do you like it?" she asked, letting her fingers glide down the seam between her sweet lips.

"Holy hell, yea, I like very much. I gotta have you, Bella, hard and fast, honey." She only nodded as he pulled her thong from her body, spreading her legs. He let his jeans drop to the floor and touched his wet tip to her hot slit. Sinking inside, he moaned with satisfaction as she arched toward him, her huge breasts spilling to the sides.

"Oh God, yes, Diego, faster, honey. You fill me up so perfectly," she smiled.

"Jesus, baby, yes, keep fucking talking," he growled.

"You like that?" Bella knew he probably liked it. Most men, she'd learned through the other women and those magnificent books, liked dirty talk. "You like when I talk about your big thick cock filling my pussy, my wet, aching pussy for you, baby. You like that?"

"Yea," he croaked like a boy going through puberty.

"Mmmm, I like it too. I like telling you how full you make me feel. I like when those big balls of yours slap against my ass. I love the sound of it, the feel of it, the feel of you spilling inside me."

"Oh shit, Bella, baby..." His body rocked against hers. The vibrations of his need and orgasm filled her senses as he hit that magical spot in her body. Her own orgasm shaking her to the core. She could hear the sounds of their wetness combined, feel the warm juices of their lovemaking flowing from her opening, down the crack of her ass.

"Holy hell, woman! That was fucking epic." Razor kissed her face, feeling his cock already hardening again inside her. "Do I owe that to those fabulous books again?"

"Maybe," she grinned. "Maybe, I'm feeling braver with you. Also, I love that the girls and I can talk about sex, and they don't make me feel stupid. We all have different experiences, and honestly, those books are helpful. But as we all know, practice makes perfect."

Bella wrapped her legs around his waist, grinding her pelvis against his hard cock, rocking her hips back and forth. She felt his cock harden inside her and grinned.

"Again, Diego, this time from behind."

CHAPTER THIRTY-ONE

Zulu and Ghost stood with the five marshals waiting for Hector Castro. Although the marshals were technically in charge of the transfer and guarding of Castro, they understood from Mike Crossing that these men would be given a wide berth considering their history. The marshals weren't stupid. They knew exactly what these men had done in their former career and would gladly allow them to take the lead.

"How long for us to get Chesapeake?" asked the young marshal. Ghost had gotten all their names, but honestly, they looked identical. All around thirty, all around six-foot, all dressed in jeans and t-shirts, although he'd had to tell them to untuck the damn things.

"Sorry, Rogers, right?" asked Ghost. The young man nodded. "We should get to the house by around six if we keep a steady speed and don't have any traffic issues. Zulu will drive, and one of you will be in the passenger seat. I'll sit in the back with Castro while the others surround us. He stays with me at all times."

The younger men nodded at Ghost, deferring to his experience. As the buzzer for the big metal door sounded, they all turned to see

Hector walking towards them in wrist and ankle chains. Two big guards flanked him, the warden walking in front of them.

"Warden, we appreciate your cooperation in this," said Zulu.

"It's not exactly cooperation," he grimaced, "it's more like coercion. I'm beginning to wonder what kinds of connections you fellas have."

"The good kind, warden, the good kind." Ghost looked toward Castro, who was watching the exchange with fascination and a small grin. "Mr. Castro? It's a pleasure to meet you. Your sister Isabella is a welcome addition to our family."

Castro looked at the two huge men, both dressed in jeans, black motorcycle boots, long-sleeved t-shirts covered in a leather kutte, and leather jacket. The older man had a beard laced with gray that might make you believe he was in his fifties, but his eyes said he was years younger. The slightly younger man was a mountain. Literally six-foot-six or bigger and layered with hard-earned muscle.

"It's a pleasure to meet you both. I'm glad to do anything I can if it helps Bella and Razor have a life together." Ghost nodded, taking the keys from the guard. He grabbed one elbow and Zulu the other, walking out into the covered yard to place him in the van.

"Why all the secrecy?" asked Hector. "I thought we wanted him to know I was out."

"We do, but on our terms and on our time," said Zulu. "Once we have both you and Bella safe in the house, we're going to have a press statement released that will say you were given a temporary furlough to see your sick sister. It will be too much for Gavin to pass up."

Castro nodded as he was helped into the van, his chains secured to the floorboards. He looked up at Zulu as if to say, is this all really necessary.

"Let's make one thing clear, Hector. You murdered six men. Now, I won't argue the semantics of them being six pieces of shit, but let's just say it is what it is. We're here to ensure that you get to that house and get back here alive. If anything happens to you, we, all of us, Diego, Bella, everyone will be held responsible. Other than keeping Bella alive, you are my number one priority, simply because I do not want anyone to pay for your mistakes.

"Now, you seem like a decent enough guy other than the whole killing six people thing. Diego likes you, and that's enough for me but make no mistake about it. You try to escape, you pull anything, anything at all, and consequences or no, I will not hesitate to put a bullet between your eyes, nor will the two snipers who will be watching you at all times." That earned a brow raise from Castro.

"Understood. I have no intentions of not fulfilling my part of this bargain. You seem to forget that everything, everything I have ever done was to protect my sister and ensure that she lives a healthy, happy life. I damn sure won't fuck that up now. You have my word." Castro extended one cuffed hand, and Zulu gripped it, shaking.

"Let's go," said Ghost. "We want to make the house before nightfall if we can."

Two hours into the drive, they stopped for a bathroom break and food, quickly getting back inside the van. The marshals showed maturity and professionalism, always watching the roads and Hector.

"Can I ask how Bella is doing?" said Castro. Ghost nodded.

"She'd doing well. She's fit in with our family, our team, well.
Zulu's wife is a brilliant doctor. Trauma surgery is really her specialty, but
she's trying to help your sister."

"Wait, what? Is Bella truly sick?" said Castro with a look of panic
on his face. Ghost felt sorry for the man in the moment. He really did
have his sister's best interest at heart.

"No, sorry, let me be clear. Gabi is helping Bella with a potential
surgery for her vision. Razor doesn't know yet. She wants to keep it
under wraps until they know whether or not it might help."

"I-I can't believe this. She might be able to see?" he whispered.
Zulu looked to the backseat and nodded.

"My wife thinks the doctors missed something. I'm not sure of
everything she knows, but just remember that we're keeping all of this
quiet until Bella wants to say something to Razor." Castro nodded but
immediately lost himself in thought.

Twenty years of fighting for his sister. Trying to help her. He'd
taken the word of the doctor and done nothing to obtain a second
opinion, mostly because they couldn't afford it. Instead, he'd relegated
himself to the fact that Isabella would be blind for the rest of her life, and

he would find a way to make sure she could function in the world of

darkness. Now, he was learning that perhaps he'd tied her to that prison

unnecessarily. How would she ever forgive him?

CHAPTER THIRTY-TWO

Gavin Baker dialed the number for Carol Jessup and received no answer. Sending a text message, he waited, hoping to receive a response. When none came, he moved on down his list to Janet Birnbaum and then Donna Viceroy. Still nothing. After sending messages to the last two of his gullible pups, Alice and Mildred, his nerves started to get the best of him. Then as if they all were responding at once, five text messages came through:

We will no longer be providing you funds for your sick twisted games. Nor we will be giving you safe haven in our homes. We've all decided to take a vacation... without you... best of luck.

"No, no, this can't be happening," he whispered to himself. "How is it possible that all of them, all five, knew something was wrong."

Baker paced inside the tiny motel room. What was he going to do now? He was down to his last two hundred dollars. The gas tank was full, but after that, he had nothing. If he continued to kidnap and rob people, he would be caught without some outside assistance.

The pre-paid phone couldn't be tracked, so how did all five get a message to him at once? Looking down, he decided to type in a reply, trying to explain things.

You don't understand. Things are not what they seem. Someone is playing games with my life. I need help if I am to survive. Please don't leave me literally in the cold.

He pressed send, and a message immediately returned.

You no longer have the ability to send text messages.

"What the hell?" he howled at the walls. Someone in the room next to him banged on the wall dividing their room, and Baker grimaced. What was happening? Who was fucking with his life? He needed to find Isabella Castro to make Hector pay for what he'd done.

He could have made him his own in prison. He wasn't happy about being any man's bitch, but Castro was a smaller man, known to at least be gentle with his lovers and give them favors. Evan Black had been almost pampered by the man in those first few years. He just wanted a little of that for himself.

Instead, he'd turned him over as a favor to Tank Garrigan, a three-hundred-and-forty-pound man with hands the size of plates. He wasn't gentle in the least, shoving his big stiff cock down his throat while forcing his mouth open. He'd enjoyed the pain, enjoyed the torment. When he would least expect it, Tank would call for him and force him to do unspeakable things to his body.

The worst was just getting fucked in the ass by the man. If he'd been gentle, like Carol had been, he wouldn't have minded. But no, Tank had to be cruel and forceful with his thick, hairy dick. When Gavin had the great idea of letting the guards know of Tank's secret stash in his room, he thought he'd be rid of the man. Instead, he was given just two weeks in solitary, and that was not enough for Baker to find protection.

Within days of him rejoining the population, he'd had his men hold him down in the laundry room and sliced his penis and testicles off, leaving him there to bleed out. Three months. Three long months in the hospital to recover from his injuries, never to be seen as a man again. Having to sit to pee. Not being able to touch a woman the way he'd desired.

Castro. He was the one at fault for all of this, and he would kill his sister and then find a way to kill him. Turning on the television, he settled against the headboard for the night, trying to make a plan.

In other news, tonight, we've learned that the notorious leader of the Desperados, Hector Castro, was released on a temporary furlough to visit his sister, who is gravely ill. Castro killed six men in cold blood, receiving two life sentences. His sister is said to reside in the Chesapeake area.

Gavin smiled at the television. Looking upwards, he said a thank you. Things were definitely looking up for him. Now, he just had to find out where in Chesapeake the sister was staying. He would find her. One way or another, he would find her.

CHAPTER THIRTY-THREE

The big house on the Chesapeake, recently remodeled by Grant and his team, was now a retreat for the Steel Patriots or, as it was being used in this case, a safe house. The back windows sprawled floor-to-ceiling along the entire back wall, giving astounding views of the bay. The new glass was bulletproof, shatter-resistant, and hurricane grade. The wood floors were warm, giving a cottage feel to the five thousand square foot property.

"Okay, so we are entering the front door, honey. How do you want to get the lay of the place?" asked Razor. Ace stepped in behind the couple, his various computers slung over his shoulder, Hawk and Eagle close behind with the bags.

"I... is Ace here?" she asked, raising her head as if searching for his scent.

"Right behind you, Isabella," he said politely.

"Last time, you were so good at explaining the layout of the restaurant and barn. Can you help me with that this time? I mean, I know you can, honey, but..."

"No problem at all," he grinned. "Seems this is definitely more of an Ace thing. I'll get our bags settled in our room and get some food and water set out for Taco." He nodded at Ace as the young man stepped forward, tentatively taking Isabella's hand. He laid it in the crook of his arm.

"If-if this isn't comfortable for you…"

"No," he said quickly. "It's fine, really. Okay, so we're facing the living room right now. There is a clear path to the open space. On the right and left are long sofas facing a television above the fireplace. If you walk approximately twelve steps, you should be able to feel the first sofa." She walked thirteen steps, feeling her shins hit something hard and unyielding and reached down to feel the fabric of the sofa.

"My steps are smaller than yours," she smiled. Ace grinned and nodded, giving a small 'yea.'

"Turning left, we walk another fifteen steps, and you'll be at the bar in the kitchen. Behind the bar will be the cabinets, stove, etc. I would say since this is short-term, let us do the cooking." She nodded as Ace led her down the first long hallway, allowing her to feel the doorways for various bedrooms and bathrooms. They headed back toward the kitchen, which she maneuvered around by herself, and then down another long hallway where the master bedroom and two guest rooms were.

"This door here leads to a safe room in the basement," he said, opening the door. He flipped on the light, obviously for him, not her, and walked down the stairs, careful to allow her to feel the steps first. Taco was right behind them. "You're at the bottom of the stairs now, Isabella. If you turn right and walk ten paces, you're going to feel the steel door for the safe room."

She did as he instructed, and sure enough, she found the saferoom door. She felt for the handle and pulled.

"The room has two cots on each side, a small refrigerator which has been stocked, and a two-way radio. To get into the room, you would have to have a code for the door, which only we have. Once you go inside, close it, and secure the door by simply pressing the button on the left." He held her hand, gently guiding it to feel for the button. She nodded, and he let her hand slide back down to her side as he rubbed his own against his jeans.

"I know this is hard for you, Ace. Thank you."

"It's not as difficult as I thought it would be," he said, staring at the woman. "I've been trying to get better, venture out more. I'm working with both Bree and Gabi on some techniques, and Taylor and Darby are both really patient with me. We do this exercise a few times a week where we either just sit and touch hands or walk and touch hands. I never thought I'd be able to do even that, and now I can. Who knows, maybe one day a woman is in my future?" he said with a disbelieving tone.

"There's not a thing wrong with you, Ace. Nothing. You know, in many ways I have an advantage from others. By not being able to see the ugliness in the world, I don't experience things the way others do. If my childhood had been like yours, I might be afraid of certain sounds instead of touch. As it is, I have trouble with being in new places or removed from anything that has become my normal environment. I'm a creature of habit all the way."

"I can see that. I can't imagine having your sight and then losing it. It seems beyond cruel. You know, I've had a few dates and explained to women why I have to take things so slowly, do things, uh, in a different way." She only nodded, no sense of disgust or judgment.

"You'll find someone, Ace; I just know it. I have a sixth sense about these things." Ace actually chuckled at the statement, and for a moment, Bella wasn't sure what that sound was.

"I do believe if anyone has a sixth sense, it would be you, Bella. Ready to walk this through again?" he asked.

"As I'll ever be. Lead the way, my fearless guide," she said, taking his arm. And for the first time in his life, for Ace, it felt like the most natural thing in the world.

CHAPTER THIRTY-FOUR

Ghost opened the door to the house, and Zulu followed with Castro glued to his hip. One of the marshals moved the van so that it could easily be seen from the main road. The other vehicles were all secured in the massive five-car garage. Ace stood and nodded at his friends, seeing Hector Castro and the resemblance to his sister.

"I'll take the marshals and show them their rooms," said Ace.

Ghost nodded a thank you and then led Hector toward the sofa. Sitting him down. As Isabella came down the long hallway, he grinned at the woman being closely followed by Taco. He watched her lips counting steps in the hallway, feeling for the rooms on her left and right, when finding one, smiling to herself that she got it right.

"Bella? It's Ghost and Zulu. We're here with your brother," he said. She quickened her steps and then stopped at the kitchen, feeling for the bar and carefully maneuvering around the huge island.

"Hector?"

"I'm here, Izzy," he said, smiling at his sister. She heard the clanging of chains and grimaced.

"Why is he chained?" she asked.

"Izzy, it's okay," he said. "Come here and give me a hug. You look beautiful, hermana." He pulled his sister in for a hug, kissing her cheek as Razor came into view.

"Hector, nice to see you," said Razor.

"I doubt that," grinned the other man, "but we're here to make sure our Bella is safe, and if I can do that, then all is right in the world." Zulu walked toward Hector with the keys for his chains and started to unlock them.

"What are you doing?" asked Pulaski, one of the marshals.

"The man is in an armed, locked-down house. I'm not going to make him shuffle to take a piss. He's given us his word, and I don't believe for one fucking minute he's doing anything to put his sister in harm's way. So, while he's in this house, he will be unchained. You good with that, son?" said Zulu, staring the younger man down.

"Yes, sir." He looked at the other marshals and shrugged, not willing to fight the big man on that issue.

"So now what?" asked another marshal, Vernon. "How will Baker know where to find her... him?"

"We've given him a specific area to search," said Ghost. "Ace is going to watch the cameras in the little villages around this area. Once we know he's close, we'll send Isabella and two men into town to pick up a prescription, sort of. Baker won't be able to resist. He'll either make a move or follow, but either way, we're going to be ready for him."

Eagle stepped through the back sliding-glass door and shook from the frigid air, his rifle slung over his back. He looked up to see a group of faces he knew and a group of unknown faces staring back at him.

"Everyone, this is Eagle. Eagle and his twin Hawk are our snipers. The fucking best at what they do. They never, and I do mean never, miss. One of them will have eyes on this house at all times. You boys okay out there?" he asked.

"Peachy," said Eagle. "The duck blind we're using actually has a small space heater. We're layered up, so we should be fine. I just came in to get some food and supplies."

"Wait!" said Bella. "Are they sleeping out there? They can't sleep outside. There has to be another way. They're going to freeze to death out there." Castro smiled at his sister's tender heart, shaking his head.

Chances were pretty good that these men had slept in places a helluva lot worse than some damn duck blind.

"Bella, I sure wish I would have gotten to you first. You'd realize I'm far more handsome and hung than Razor," said Eagle, walking past the woman. She let out a small snicker, and Razor slapped the back of Eagle's head. He filled a backpack with waters and food and then headed back outside.

"We'll be fine, Bella, I promise. We're warm out there, and besides, nothing more important right now than keeping you alive." He kissed her cheek as he walked by, earning him a growl from Razor. "You know, if I were my brother, I'd deserve that growl, but I'm the decent one. Remember that."

"Which, by the way," said Ghost, "later I want to know why your brother flashed his dick to a senior citizen stripper." Castro nearly spit out his water while the gasps of the marshals from behind him echoed in the room. Razor, Ace, and Zulu all just shook their heads, smiling.

"Oh, that. It's a long story, but let's just say it was necessary." Ghost nodded, and Eagle disappeared into the marsh.

"One day, Hawk is going to either get his dick cut off, or he's going to find a woman that he'd be willing to cut it off for. I just hope I'm alive to see it. Bella? Remember the rules. You don't leave the house, not for any reason. I don't care if we've all been taken, if he's threatening one of us. You do not leave. Is that understood?" he asked.

"Yes, yes, that's clear," she said, nodding in his direction.

"Okay, I'm going to make us some dinner and see what kind of trouble we can find. Ace, keep eyes on the cameras and let us know if anything pops up. The rest of you, regular patrols on the property. We keep tight communication in my team, so I expect check-ins every ten minutes." The marshals all nodded as they went about their business.

Bella took the seat next to her brother and reached for his hand.

"So, tell me, Bella, when will you be getting married and having babies?"

CHAPTER THIRTY-FIVE

Gavin Baker felt as though he were looking for a needle in a haystack. Isabella Castro could be anywhere along the Chesapeake, which meant Hector could be anywhere as well. He started making his way along the Chesapeake scenic route, but the truth was it was over four hundred miles of byway that led from the upper Maryland coastal areas to the most southern.

He needed to speed this process up, and perhaps flashing a few photos of Isabella around would help. Stopping in the first small town, he asked around in coffee shops, boutiques, and finally pharmacies, hoping that perhaps if she were ill, she may have gone into one.

Spending almost all of his money, he was finally left with no choice but to rob an older couple outside a grocery store, stealing more than three hundred dollars in cash and their credit cards. He left them tied up in the car, to be found hopefully by someone soon.

As darkness approached, he discovered a small motel on the side of the road and purchased a room for the night. Across the street was a seafood restaurant and bar. Pulling a baseball cap over his face, he entered the restaurant, taking a seat near the front for easy escape.

To his left was a woman in a dress that was much too revealing for someone her age. She looked lonely and was definitely on drink three or four by the looks of her lazy eyes. Gavin watched the woman for a few moments, and then deciding he needed a distraction, he made his move.

"Good evening," he said, sitting in the seat next to her.

"Hi."

"Can I buy you another drink?" he asked.

"Oh, no thanks, I'm waiting on someone."

Sure you are, he thought. They all say that, but they're not really. In reality, they're waiting on him to take them away from their miserable existence. He let a hand slide up her arm, and she looked down at him, her face masked with disgust.

"What the hell is wrong with you?" she yelled loud enough for the bar to hear. "I said I was waiting for someone!"

"Hey, bitch," he growled, "you were coming on to me. I saw the way you looked at me when I sat down. I know what that look means."

"Have you lost your senses?" she sneered. "I have no interest in you whatsoever. I'm waiting on my husband, who went to the restroom."

A large shadow appeared by her side, and Gavin looked up at the big beefy man.

"Problem, honey?" he asked.

"Yea, this pervert came on to me and wouldn't take 'no' for an answer," she huffed. Gavin started to stand, but the man pushed him back down on the stool.

"No trouble in here," said the bartender.

"Ain't gonna be no trouble as long as this piece of shit apologizes to my wife," he said.

Gavin looked at the man and then back at the woman, a smirk gracing her disgusting lips. He had enough trouble. He didn't need more, but he wasn't about to let her get away with this. Standing, he tossed a twenty on the bar and nodded in the direction of the man and woman.

"Sorry I tried to pick up your whore."

He almost made it to the door before all hell broke loose. Fists flew, barstools were tossed, and screaming could be heard above the roar of police vehicles as Gavin made an exit out the back door, circling around to head across the street to his room. He happily watched the foray from his room, laughing as the big man and his wife were carted off in the back of the police car.

That'll serve them right for trying to outsmart me. Now, a good night's rest, and tomorrow will be my lucky day.

CHAPTER THIRTY-SIX

"It's our lucky day," said Ace. "He was seen on video camera last night at Peak Oyster House. He started a scuffle with another patron and then got out the backdoor, but I picked him up on the outside cameras. He's staying at this little motel about twenty minutes from here. He's in our backyard."

Razor looked at Bella and then back to Ghost and Zulu.

"It's showtime, baby. You ready?" he asked. She nodded her head and walked to the bedroom. Using the powder Grace had given her, she carefully brushed it on her face, hoping she was obtaining the right amount of 'ghastly' to give Gavin the impression she was ill.

Ghost and Zulu took the front seat, Razor and Bella the backseat, making their way toward the motel they knew that Gavin was staying in. Once close, they slowed, trying to spot him.

"He's looking for me," said Bella. "I need to be seen. Take me inside a few businesses. Maybe a restaurant, a gas station, places he would be. It doesn't have to be for long, just enough to give him a clear view of my face." Razor looked into the front seat and nodded.

"You know I can hear you nod, right?" she said with her arms folded across her chest.

"I... you're going to have to teach me that trick, baby," smiled Razor as he kissed her cheek. "Sorry, honey, we just aren't used to having to say everything out loud. You may not hear us communicate if something happens, but rest assured we're here, and we are."

"I get it. Really, I do. Just remember you can't look at me and nod or hold up a few fingers and expect I'll know what you're saying. You have to somehow verbally communicate with me."

"Do you know Morse code?" asked Zulu.

"Yes," she smiled. "It was one of the first non-verbal pieces of communication they taught us in school. If you tapped out a message, I would understand."

"Alright, I'll make sure we send a code if we need to," said Zulu. "Convenience store next to his motel. Let's go in there and spend a minute or two."

They pulled up to the pumps and filled the tank, although it needed less than fifteen dollars worth of gas. Inside, Isabella gripped Razor's arm, following him up and down the aisles. They bought a few snack items and some soda, casually paying for the items at the checkout counter. Walking back to the vehicle, Razor stood outside the door with Isabella for a few minutes, scanning the area behind his sunglasses.

Less than a half-mile down the road was a small diner. Although no one was particularly hungry, they entered the diner asking for a table for four. Seated away from the windows and doors, it was Zulu's big body plastered against Bella in the seat.

"Why are you sitting next to me and not Razor?" she asked quietly.

"I think I might be hurt by that," he grinned. "Cuz I'm a bigger barrier, honey. He can't get to you through me."

"You're not bulletproof, Zulu. I don't want anything happening to you or Ghost. I could never forgive myself if I had to go back and tell Grace or Gabi something happened here all because of me."

"First of all," said Ghost, "nothing is because of you. It's because of Gavin Baker and a little bit because of your brother." Bella nodded.

"Yea, I'm trying to reconcile myself to that."

"Secondly, we all know the risks of these assignments, Bella. We take them eyes wide open and gladly for our brothers. Grace and Gabi both know the risks."

"And will you take the same risks?" she asked, turning her head toward Razor. "When this is done, if something like this happens in the future, will you take the same risks?"

"I will, baby," said Razor, reaching for her hand. "Not gonna lie to you about that. It's what we do as a team, protect one another, and what's important to us." She nodded, nibbling on her lower lip, and then felt Zulu stiffen next to her. She sensed that they were nodding at one another or signaling but was too frightened to say anything.

Then a soft tapping on the table made her ears perk. Gavin... entered... appear sick... say nothing.

Let the games begin.

CHAPTER THIRTY-SEVEN

There she was, just sitting there with three men, looking pathetically pale and sickly. The men were all large, much bigger than him, but then again, he was trained and intelligent. It was unlikely that these men would be able to fend him off once he got them on his turf.

For now, he was happy to see Isabella Castro. He would follow the men back to where they were staying and, no doubt, where Hector was now located. The foursome finished their coffee and left a twenty on the table, sliding from the booth. The big black man kept his arm firmly around Isabella, looking as though she could barely hold herself upright. She would be fun to take in her weakened state. If things went as planned, he would eliminate the three men and then force Hector to watch him kill his sister.

He followed a few cars behind the big SUV as they wound their way through the parkway and down several long dirt roads until they reached the massive house facing the water. The car parked out front, and just as predicted, Hector rushed out to envelop his sister in a hug.

"Perfect!" he whispered to himself. Now I'll wait until dark and then move in. This will be a piece of cake. Just eliminate the

Neanderthals and then take down Castro, but not before he gets to watch poor Isabella take her final breath.

He scanned the horizon to see if there were any additional men and saw no one. He would be done with this and then find a new life for himself. Perhaps he'd go to the West Coast, or south, somewhere warm. He'd heard about a doctor in Mexico who might be able to give him new genitals. He wondered how much that would cost? It didn't matter. He'd find someone willing to give him the money, or he'd simply take it.

That's exactly what he would do. Finish this with Castro and make his way to Mexico. Then again, he still had unfinished business with his brother. Bastard sold him out, wouldn't even vouch for him the way brothers were supposed to do. Maybe he could swing through Atlanta and end that nasty business, then make his way toward Mexico. In fact, he was certain his brother had a stash of money somewhere. If he could torture that bit of information out of him, it would be even better.

He looked back at the house one more time and around the property. It was nearly sunset. Soon darkness would ascend, and it would be his time to finally have revenge.

Yes, indeed, today was his lucky day.

CHAPTER THIRTY-EIGHT

"Listen to me, honey," said Razor. "You're going to sit out here in the living room having a casual cup of tea with your brother, all snuggly wrapped up. When Hawk and Eagle tell us he's seen you, you're going to get up with Taco and make your way down the hall as if you're not feeling well. Zulu and I will be sitting out here with Hector."

"Wh-what about the rest of the men? The marshals, where will they be?"

"Don't worry, baby. They're all going to be here. Ace will be downstairs in the basement, the last line of defense in case Gavin somehow gets passed us all. But listen to me, baby, he will not get passed any of us. Once he is in the living room, Hawk and Eagle will have him in their sights."

"But... but you said it was bulletproof glass," she said.

"Smart girl," chuckled Zulu. "It is, honey, but they have armor-piercing bullets. Gavin won't leave this house." She nodded and took her seat as instructed on the sofa. Hector next to her, simply holding her hand.

"Talk like you would any other time. Don't try too hard," said Razor.

"Tell me about where you live now, Bella," said Castro.

"Oh, it's wonderful, Hector. I've been doing all my classes online, so I'll still finish school on time. I'm still not sure what I'm going to do afterwards, but I'll figure that out soon enough. Anyway, it's an amazing place. All the wives, they've been so kind to me, just treating me like a sister right away. I like being around them. I've never had a lot of female friends, and they're all amazing, Hector."

"You love this place," he stated.

"I do," she smiled. "The children are so wonderful, and George, he's this older veteran that helps around the compound and cooks for the restaurant. He rearranged the whole kitchen so that I could go in there and cook any time I wanted to. He just met this amazing woman, Mary, and they moved in together... at their age! Can you believe it?" Hector chuckled at his sister's excitement and nodded.

"I believe it, hermana, because I think these men love like no men I've ever known. I know that Diego will protect you and love you forever.

I'm not worried about you any longer." She nodded and kissed his cheek, just resting there for a few minutes.

"Do you remember when we were children, Hector? You would bring home a video, and two nights a week, we would have brother/sister movie night. It didn't matter what else was happening in the world. You and I would have our movie nights. You would make me popcorn, and we would snuggle up on the sofa together."

"I remember, hermana. They are some of the best memories for me. They get me through my darkest days."

"No matter what happens, Hector, thank you for being an amazing big brother."

He's climbing in through the front bedroom window.

Hector heard the man speak into the microphone in his ear and gave a short nod.

"You look tired, hermana. I think you should sleep now," he said, kissing her forehead. She stood and called for Taco. Sensing a stranger, he let out a low growl, but Bella called to him to heel. Hector let a tear slip as he watched his sister walk away for perhaps the last time. Taking his seat once more, he watched Zulu and Razor, completely casual and relaxed, seated across from him.

"Wanna watch a movie, man?" asked Zulu.

"Sure," said Hector. "Anything is fine by me, as long as it's not done in a prison." The men gave a nervous laugh and then heard the sound of a weapon being cocked behind them. Razor and Zulu turned quickly, reaching for their weapons.

"I wouldn't do that if I were you," smiled Gavin. "You all thought you were so smart, thought you would get past me. No one is smarter than me. Hector, it's so good to see you."

"Why are you here, Gavin?"

"Why for Isabella, of course, and you. I'm going to take her, have some fun with her, and let you watch. Then I'm going to kill you."

"Pretty sure of yourself, little man," said Zulu, grinning at the man.

"I've got the weapon!" he yelled. Zulu nodded, pursing his lips as Razor grinned in his direction. "What are you smiling at? I. Have. The..."

The sounds of shattering glass filled the room as a bullet pierced the right shoulder of Gavin Baker, causing him to drop his weapon.

"You were saying?" said Zulu.

"No, no, I'm the smarter person," he cried. Hector walked toward the man, and Zulu looked back at Razor, wondering if they should stop him.

"You are a sick man, Gavin. I knew that the moment we met. I'm sorry Tank didn't kill you when he had the chance, but I can't allow you to walk the earth and potentially put my sister in danger." Castro bent to pick up the gun, and Razor called to him.

"Hector! Don't do this, brother. Don't!"

"I have to," he whispered. "Remember your promise to me." He lifted the weapon and pulled the trigger, firing three shots into Gavin Baker, but not before Marshal Pulaski fired twice into Hector Castro.

Ghost ran into the room, followed by two other marshals, looking down at the bodies.

"Fuck!" he yelled. "Call Mike." Razor raced to the backroom for Isabella, pulling her by the hand to say goodbye to her brother.

"Wh-what is that sound? Someone is gasping for air. Who..."

"Iz-Izzy."

"Oh God," she said, kneeling on the floor, crawling to the sound. She reached a hand out, finding her brother's foot, and cried out. "Hector, hermano, no, no..."

"I had to, Izzy. You're safe now. You're safe. Live, my hermana... live..."

Bella gripped her brother into a fierce hug, oblivious to the blood seeping into her own clothes. The sounds of sirens could be heard in the distance, but they would be too late for Hector Castro and definitely too late for Gavin Baker.

Mike Crossing smoothed things over with the warden. No one anticipated that Hector would die in this mission, only that he would be used. Of course, it was also unexpected that he would shoot Baker after he'd already been stopped. Perhaps things work out as they should.

Late the following afternoon, the team pulled into the compound, glad to be home and away from any potential danger. Bella immediately went to her room and to bed. Razor tried to speak with her but just couldn't seem to get through. Each of the women took turns over the next few days, but no one could seem to draw her out.

On day three, Razor was about at his wits end when he walked toward their suite, only to find that the door was open, and Ace was seated next to Bella, holding her hand.

"He did it because he loved you, Isabella. I know it doesn't feel that way, but one day when you're rocking babies with Razor, you'll see that I'm right."

"If he loved me, he wouldn't have left me," said Bella.

"He left you a long time ago, Isabella," said Ace. "He left you the day he killed those six gang members. He knew then that he would never see the other side of the prison walls. He did this, like he did everything in his life, to keep you safe. Don't disrespect him for that, Isabella. It was all he had to give to you, and I think that's a pretty amazing legacy."

Ace said nothing else, just sat there holding Isabella's hand. She finally nodded and stood, taking his elbow.

"Will you take me downstairs for lunch?" she asked. He made a soft sound of agreement, and as they walked through the door, he looked toward Razor and said nothing. In the restaurant, the women swarmed Isabella and hugged her, kissing her cheeks, comforting her.

"I'm okay now, I think," she said, smiling at the group. "Gabi? Do you think we could make that trip to Baltimore like we planned?"

"I do, honey. I'll make the arrangements. We'll tell the boys we're Christmas shopping. With any luck, we can have this done Monday, be back on Tuesday, and you can celebrate Thanksgiving the way we hoped."

"I can't believe this," she whispered. "I have a tiny sliver of hope that I'll see. I just can't believe it."

"Well, let's get all our ducks in a row. After all, we want this to be a surprise for Razor if we can manage to keep it quiet." The girls huddled together at the table, making plans while the men watched them all laughing.

"What are they scheming now?" asked Whiskey.

"No telling," said Razor, "but I don't give a shit. I'd let them scheme to take over the government if it kept that smile on Bella's face. Ace? You're a miracle worker, brother." Ace nodded at his friend with a small grin.

"Who knew the dysfunctional, inept guy with no skills whatsoever with the female population could be so handy?" he said with a small grin. Razor frowned at the man, as did the other men at the table.

"Brother, who the fuck ever said you were dysfunctional or inept? You are the most 'ept and functional of us all, Ace. You're the only one that can remove his emotions from the situation when needed and see things clearly. I wouldn't change a fucking thing about anything you do."

Ace nodded again, giving a small smile to his friends. Coming towards their table was Mike Crossing, looking smug.

"Gentlemen, I believe the agreement was that nothing would happen to Hector Castro."

"Hello to you too, Mike," said Ghost. "We did agree to that. However, we didn't control Gavin Baker. Besides, the agreement was Castro wouldn't escape or harm anyone else. He didn't."

"Agree to disagree," he said with a grin. "Either way, you broke the agreement and owe me one." Ghost started to protest when he held up his hands. "I have a situation in North Dakota." As the men shuffled their feet nervously, it was Ace that stepped up sure-footed.

"Is this like the school for girls?" he asked. All eyes turned to Ace, their faces filled with confusion and anger.

"What did you say, young man?" asked Mike Crossing.

"It was a simple question, Admiral. Is this going to be like the mission with the girls at the school? You know, the mission that caused everyone to be forced into retirement."

"Be careful what you say, son," said Mike.

"I'm not your son, and I am no longer under your command. You see, I'm good at my job, excellent in fact, which is why you removed me as the intelligence operative on that mission and replaced me with your pathetically inept nephew."

"What. The. Fuck?" growled Ghost.

"You don't know what you're talking about," said Crossing in a low register.

"But I do. I'm not so ignorant as to make statements like that without proof. Wesley Hubbard, the only son of your sister. He was trying to make a name for himself with the intelligence community, and, of course, he did. It just wasn't the name you wanted. The problem was, you knew that I was tracking the information he was feeding to the team.

He didn't find those girls. I did. He didn't know where the terrorists had gone. I did. I fed him that information, hoping he would get it to the team in time, but of course, he was an idiot and couldn't seem to manage that task."

Mike Crossing was seething, staring at the younger man. He'd known he was brilliant, genius-level capable in multiple disciplines of hand-to-hand, computers, and other electronics, but he'd promised he would find a way for his nephew to get in the door. And he did. At the expense of this team.

"It's done. None of it matters now."

"It all matters, and it really matters to Wesley, now a candidate for the sixtieth congressional district in Georgia. It would be a shame for all that information to come to light just as his political career is coming into its own."

"You're lying," he whispered. Ghost stepped forward and looked straight into Ace's eyes, nodding with a small grin.

"Fucking awesome," he said, gripping the younger man's shoulder. "I believe you're done here, Mike. Don't call us again."

"You'll need me one day. You'll need something from me, and I'll get it for you because then you'll owe me."

"Not likely," said Razor.

Crossing looked at the group of men and then at Ace, nodding.

"You're even better than I thought." He walked back out into the night and, hopefully, out of their lives.

"Dysfunctional?" said Razor, smiling. "I think fucking not."

CHAPTER THIRTY-NINE

"Call us when you check into the hotel and when you leave tomorrow," said Ghost to Grace and the rest of the women.

"Honey, we'll be fine. We're just doing some holiday shopping, and then we'll be back. Don't worry." Kissing their men goodbye, the women made the trip to Baltimore early Monday morning, arriving with ten minutes to spare for Bella's appointment. Waiting patiently in the outer room, they were all crossing their fingers in hopes that it was something that could be fixed.

Gabi and another woman appeared from the back, but no Bella.

"What's going on?" asked Darby.

"It's treatable," said Gabi, smiling. "She has what we refer to as a floating tumor behind her eyes. It can easily be missed unless you know what you're looking for. It's why she could see some light and color. It's not permanent. They're prepping her now. In two hours, she'll be done, and then we can take her back to the hotel. By tomorrow afternoon, I can remove her bandages, and we'll know just how much she can actually see."

"Oh my God," whispered Taylor. "I can't believe it. That poor girl has lived twenty years like this."

"I know, honey, but she'll get a lifetime with her vision now."

"Wow, should we call Razor?" asked Kat.

"No, Bella wants it to remain a surprise, and she's still uncertain if this is all real." She turned to see her friend signaling to her that they were ready. "I'm going to sit in on the surgery. I'll let you guys know when we're done." They all hugged Gabi, telling her to hug and kiss Bella for them.

"Should we, maybe, at least buy a few things so the guys don't get suspicious?" asked Taylor.

"Shit, maybe," said Darby. "I can tell you I know Gunner will track my credit cards to see where I am."

"There's a mall connected to the hospital by catwalk. Why don't Grace, Darby, and I go over and pick up some things for the kids, and then we'll be back before the surgery is done," said Bree. They all nodded as the three women took off to do their power shopping, returning to the room just as Gabi stepped out in her scrubs.

"We think it was completely successful," she smiled. "We'll know for sure by tomorrow afternoon, but it appears that Bella will be able to see everything."

There was a collective sigh of relief as the women held one another and then waited for Bella to be released. In the hotel room, they watched movies, ordered room service, and even listened to the audio version of the next six chapters of CC Robat's book.

"Okay, I've changed my mind," said Kat. "That voice on the audiobook is hot!" Bella laughed with the women, and then when they spoke of her brother, she cried through her bandages, finally falling asleep in one another's arms.

Early the next morning, the doctor arrived at the hotel to help Gabi remove the bandages from Bella. As the women watched, Bella held her breath.

Stepping back from her, Gabi and the others waited patiently.

"Well?"

CHAPTER FORTY

"The girls should be here any time now," said Ghost. "Ace is tracking the car and their phones."

"Should we tell them at some point that we know every move they make?" asked Razor. "I mean, it seems kind of shitty to not let them know we were tracking them."

"No," said Zulu. "I'm just pissed Gabi didn't tell me she was visiting old colleagues at John's Hopkins. I mean, what if it was a man?"

"Dude, your wife fucking loves you. Don't be so insecure. It's unattractive," said Hawk.

Walking through the doors to a chorus of laughter were the women, loaded down with bags and suitcases. Last through the door was Bella with Gabi. The women were all smiling, and the guys looked at them and then one another.

"What the fuck is happening here? Why are they all grinning like that?" asked Gunner.

Bella and Gabi walked forward, Gabi holding Bella's elbow as they always did. She stopped in the center of the room and just stood there. Razor started to move toward them, but Gabi shook her head.

"Baby…"

"I like the shirt, Diego. Blue is a good color for you. You're even more handsome than I thought you would be. Hawk, I love the color of your hair. Ace, you have blue eyes. I knew it," she smiled. Ace grinned and nodded.

"You like… what… how the fuck…"

"I didn't want to tell you," she said, walking closer to him. Her eyes were red, the surrounding area irritated and dry, but she was seeing everything crystal clear. "Gabi, she knew someone. Someone genius. It was treatable. All this time, I could have been seeing. Hector never got to see… see me seeing." She laughed.

"Oh, baby," said Razor, hugging her to his chest. "Oh my God, you can see. You can see everything. Wait, what if you don't like the way I look." Bella laughed at the man who would soon be her husband and smiled.

"I loved the way you look when I couldn't see, Diego. I damn sure like the way you look when I can see," she said, kissing him.

"No jostling or moving too fast for a few days," said Gabi. "She has some drops that have to be put in her eyes four times a day and antibiotics. Other than that, we'll take her back to see the doctor in about six months unless there are issues."

"Gabi," choked Razor, pulling the woman into his arms. "Angel eyes, you gave my Angel her eyes back. How do I ever repay that?"

"Live happily," she smiled, kissing his cheek. "Love and live happily. Lord knows you both deserve it, for God's sake."

"Okay," George walking out into the big room, "enough of all this mushiness. Let's eat!"

It was hours later that Razor held Isabella in his arms, kissing her sweetly after tasting her sweet pussy on his lips. He refused to have sex because he didn't want to jostle her, but he was more than happy to give her some enjoyment. Now, his woman was in his arms.

"Diego? Can we build a house here?" she asked quietly. He leaned on one arm, looking down at her face. Unlike before, she turned, staring directly into his eyes.

"Baby, we can do whatever you want. If you want to stay here, we stay here. If you want to build a house on the property, we'll do it. I have money. Tell me what you want."

"I-I want a house. Like a cottage, I think. All white with shutters and a big porch and lots of windows so I can see everything. I want four bedrooms, one for us and one for each of our children."

"So, we're having three, are we?" he smiled.

"Yes, maybe more, but three for sure. I want a studio. A studio where I can continue to edit braille text. I know I don't have to, but it's so important. I want to design, use my engineering degree, but do it from here. I don't want to ever leave here without you," she whispered.

"Baby, you don't have to go anywhere, but the whole world is out there for you now. We could travel and see places you've always wanted to see." She shook her head slowly.

"This is the only place I ever wanted to see, and now that I have, I never want to leave it."

CHAPTER FORTY-ONE

Thanksgiving again at the Steel Patriots, and the family had almost doubled this year. There was more food, more noise, more celebration, and more weddings.

Ice and Amanda were a couple, but both agreed they would hold off a bit for the wedding until she was finished with school, and they knew for certain that she would be happy teaching music above the bookstore.

Taylor and Tango married, as did Diego and Bella, as predicted. The surprise for the group happened when Ghost and Grace stood to give their usual toasts.

"Another year, brothers," he said, staring at his men. "We're bigger; we're stronger; we're more loved, and I couldn't be happier for each one of you. Women we love, children at our feet. I never thought we would have any of this, and now here we are. I'm thankful as fu... fudge," he said, looking at Calla.

"Thank you, Uncle Ghost."

'You're welcome, angel," he grinned. "Thankful for all of you, thankful that we have two new wives joining the group, and two babies. Kat and Bree due in April."

"Three," said Grace.

"Honey, it's just Kat and Bree," he said, smiling. Grace looked up at him nibbling on her lower lip. "No, you, no…"

"Saying no doesn't make it not true, Ghost. I'm pregnant. Again."

"I'm gonna be seventy and have kids at my feet," he said, taking his seat. Grace sat on his lap, kissing his face as he stared at his son chewing on a piece of bread.

"Last one, baby," she said, smiling, "I promise. We can thank CC Robat for all of this."

"Here, here!" yelled the women. The guys all looked at them and shook their heads.

"What?" said Gabi. "I, for one, am eternally grateful for the writing. I am inspired on more than one night by the detail of the books."

"Same here," said Taylor, smiling in their direction. "Whoever CC Robat is, I owe them a huge thank you for expanding my repertoire."

"Okay, okay," said George. "Time to eat. We can talk romance books later."

"Don't you dare discount them, George," said Mary. "What we did last weekend was inspired by the wonderful mind of CC." George's jaw dropped, and the entire table broke out in laughter. Hours later, as they all left and headed home, Ace stared at the stack of books on his bedside table and finally relented.

Opening the first book, he read for three hours, unable to put it down. Over the next week, he devoured the books by CC Robat and then had a brilliant idea. One of many, but perhaps this would be his best.

EXCERPT from ACE

Dear CC Robat,

My apologies for the lack of formality, but since I'm unsure of whether to say Mr. Robat or Ms./Miss/Mrs. Robat, I'm covering my bases. You are a difficult person to find, and finding people is my job, so that's saying a lot.

My name is Alex Mills, and I'm a member of a motorcycle club called the Steel Patriots. I suppose I should back up just a bit.

I was a member of the United States Navy, part of Naval Intelligence supporting Special Forces overseas. My role was to extend critical information to my team to support them in missions, and I did. Unfortunately, during our last mission, I couldn't be with the team, and things didn't go as planned. But as with any team, we move as one, and they blamed me for nothing, trying to relieve me of the burden I felt for not having been there to support them.

My entire team retired, as did I a year later. Then we formed the motorcycle club. But we do more than just ride bikes. We help the underdogs; we rescue trafficked and abused women and children. We run a successful restaurant and bar, a custom motorcycle and auto shop, a clinic which supports our community, and so much more.

My teammates over the last two years have met the women they want to spend their lives with. They've married, had children, or will very soon. They've fallen in love and, in the process, changed my world. You see, although I am part of this amazing team, I am always somewhat on the periphery. By choice.

It's a rather sordid tale, but I don't do well with crowds or touching, so I usually sit at the edge. I'm getting better. I'm trying, but I see the relationships that my friends have, and it makes me very happy for them. Gunner, one of my teammates, is married to Darby. She owns the local bookstore.

You see, Grace, another wife, is crazy for your books. She buys them, shares them with the other wives, and they all discuss the... sex scenes. My teammates were so shocked by the changes in their wives when they found out it was because of your books they started reading them all as well.

So, all that to get to my point. I'd like you to come to Club Steel for Christmas. I know it's short notice and all, but if you could do a book signing at the Page Turner and then just spend the holiday with us, it would be extremely important to my teammates and their wives.

If you have your own family, obviously, they are invited as well. I am giving this gift to all of them so they can personally thank you, so I will cover all of your expenses. Tell me where you're flying from, and I can book the ticket or simply reimburse you. Our property has a guest cottage, and I will make sure it's available for you and whoever might be traveling with you.

I'm sure this is an insane request. I only hope that you know I'm doing this because I want to show my teammates and their wives what they mean to me. I want to give them something that will be unforgettable, and your books have given them all so much ummm, joy. (You can't tell, but I'm smiling).

Please let me know at your earliest convenience.

Regards,

Alex Mills

OTHER BOOKS BY MARY KENNEDY YOU

MIGHT ENJOY!

REAPER Security Series
Erin's' Hero
Lauren's Warrior
Lena's' Mountain
Sara's' Chance
Mary's Angel
Kari's Gargoyle
Rachelle's Savior
Adele's Heart
Tori's' Secret
Finding Lily
Montana Rules
Savannah Rain
Gray Skies
My First Choice
Three Wishes
Second Chances
One Day at a Time
When You Least Expect It
Missing Hearts
Trail of Love

Steel Patriots MC Series
Ghost – Book One
Doc – Book Two
Whiskey – Book Three
Zulu – Book Four
Gunner – Book Five
Tango – Book Six

My SEAL Boys (connections to the REAPER Series)
Ian
Noa
Carter
Lars
Trevor
Fitz
Chris
O'Hara

Strange Gifts Series
Dark Visions
Dark Medicine
Dark Flame

ABOUT THE AUTHOR

Mary Kennedy is the mother of two adult children, has an amazing son-in-law, and is grandmother to two beautiful grandsons. She works full-time at a job she loves, and writing is her creative outlet. She lives in Texas and enjoys traveling, reading, and cooking. Her passion for assisting veterans and veteran causes comes from a strong military family background. Mary loves to hear from her readers and encourages them to join her mailing list, as she'll keep you up-to-date on new releases at https://insatiableink.squarespace.com. You can also join her Facebook page at Insatiable Ink.

Dear Readers,

I love hearing from you and encourage you to visit my website Insatiable Ink. Leave me know your thoughts and ideas on new books or expanding on characters. It's also a safe space to give your own feelings, like those of the characters. I love reading about how you relate to the stories because as we all know, there's a little of each of them within us.

I look forward to hearing from you and hope you enjoy other books in my collections.

Explore... and enjoy!

www.ingramcontent.com/pod-product-compliance
Lightning Source LLC
Chambersburg PA
CBHW071457170626
46811CB00007B/2611